BAD UNION

THE WINSTON BROTHERS
BOOK ONE

DORI PULITANO

Cover designed by Taylored Designs
Editor: Striding Ibis Editing

Author Dori Pulitano
First Printing: June 2022

Quote

You can let the darkness swallow you whole, locking yourself in its hold, or you can be the light, defying the lies as you stand bright.

— KAYLEE STEPKOSKI

PROLOGUE

Drake

Sounds all too familiar fill the desolate hallway outside my door. The screams from my mother's lips pierce my chest in a way that leaves me breathless. I want to help her... want to stop the madness that's happening.

But what can *I* do? I'm only a child.

A child that shouldn't have to face such horrific events. Yet, here I am, lying on my bed, praying. Praying my brothers are hidden somewhere safe. I can't bear the thought of them enduring any more violence. Gage is the oldest and usually takes the brunt of my father's rage. A rage that's left us all battered, broken and bruised. But I don't know how much more he can take. Or any of us, for that matter. The perfect rich family to the outside world. We're the family that lives in the luxurious house everyone wishes they owned, but behind closed doors, we're trapped in a hell that's dark and dangerous. No amount of money will ever make us whole—not when the keeper of the damned uses it as a weapon. Growing up rich doesn't mean shit when your father's an abusive prick.

"Mom?" Gage's voice echoes against the pretentious art hanging on the walls outside my door. My stomach clenches knowing he's out there *alone*. The thought he'll suffer yet another fist from dear old dad, makes me bristle beneath my covers.

"Gage, baby." My mother sounds so helpless. "Go back to your room."

"Please, mom. Come with me. We can lock the door."

"Boy." The gruff sound of my father cuts him off. "Mind your damn business and get the fuck out of mine. This is between me and your mother."

"No. You're nothing but a bully. Why don't you just leave?"

The unmistakable sound of flesh being struck permeates my ears. My eyes squeeze shut in disgust.

"What the hell?!? *Gage*." My mother gasps. "Frank, stop it. He's your son, for Christ's sake."

"He'll learn not to interfere in grown-up matters. Won't you, boy?"

A scuffling noise has me straining to hear. My mother grunts and screams just before a loud thud has me crawling out from my hiding spot. I glance at the wooden barrier shielding me from the chaos, contemplating whether I should open it and step out when my bathroom door opens to reveal a scared and confused Roland. He's the youngest of us Winston boys and doesn't fully understand the dynamics of our family. Thankfully, Dad leaves Roland alone. It's a small blessing, though he uses me or Gage as his punching bag instead... when he isn't beating our mother.

"Hey, buddy." I move toward him and place my hand on his shoulder. "Did the yelling wake you?"

"Yeah. Why is dad angry at Gage?"

"I dunno. Come on, let's get in the bed."

I turn on my radio, trying to drown out the sounds in the hall. Roland and I climb onto my mattress and pull the covers around our bodies. At twelve years old, I feel more like his parental figure than his brother. Roland was a late surprise to our family and dad was less than pleased. With eight years between us, Roland relies on me and Gage for everything. Gage and I grew up fast when he came into the world. We had to. We do everything we can to help our mom keep him happy—because if he isn't happy, dad isn't happy.

And that means mom is going to pay.

The sound of screaming over the music has me jerking upright and slinging my feet off the bed. I can hear Gage carrying on about something to do with our mother, making my gut coil with trepidation. But like most boys my age, curiosity drives me out of the bed to see.

"Stay here." I ease to a stand and move toward the door. Opening it slowly, I peek around the corner of the frame.

"Gage?"

Gage's eyes widen when he sees me standing in the open. "Go back to your room, Drake. Lock the door and don't come out. For *any* reason. Do you understand me?"

I hear the words he's saying, but my eyes are locked on the still form of our mother. She's bent in a crooked position against the wall, blood oozing from a massive gash in her head coating the once pristine gold leaf wall paper.

"Mom?" I call out, my voice cracking as my bottom lip trembles just enough to affect the tone of my voice. "*Gage?*" I look at my older brother before flicking my eyes to her lifeless body again.

"Drake." His voice warns me to move, but I can't. I'm frozen in fear.

"This is *your* fault, Gage. You did this." Our father moves into the hallway, a gun in his hand. "*You* killed your mother."

"No. *You* did that. You're a fucking monster."

"I'm your father." His voice rises as he lurches toward Gage. "I'll kill you for this."

I watch in horror as they wrestle with the gun. At seventeen, Gage has filled out nicely. My father is no match for him anymore, and Gage is *angry*. He's done standing idly by.

"Fuck you!" Gage cries out, wrenching the gun from his hand as they fall to the floor.

A loud blast echoes through the ostentatious hallway, the sound ricocheting off the numerous artwork lining the cold and dank space. Its sudden clatter makes me jump. The distinct scent of gun powder fills the space as my feet move even closer. The petulant odor assaults my gut as I move toward my brother.

"Gage!" I kneel on the carpet, my knees burrowing into something wet and sticky. "Oh, God… please don't be dead."

"Drake." Gage turns his head toward me as he rolls to his knees and pushes off the floor. His eyes widen with shock as he takes in the once unblemished carpet that's now tinted red. "Call 9-1-1."

I'm rooted to the spot, unable to move. My father is lying on his back, eyes wide and unmoving. The hollowness of his gaze tells me he's gone.

"He's dead," I mutter, my voice barely a whisper. "Dad's dead."

"Drake." Gage calls my name again. "9-1-1."

"I thought…" I push to my feet and continue to stare at the man I called my father. I should feel sadness, but all I feel is relief.

"I know, buddy. I know. But mom needs help, so go call 9-1-1."

Those words spur me into action. My feet carry me toward Gage's room, where I retrieve his cell phone and press the emergency button.

"9-1-1, where is your emergency?"

"My father's been shot, and my mom is hurt. Can you send the police and an ambulance?"

I give the operator the address and stay on the phone with her as I walk back out to the hallway. Gage is bent over my mom, doing CPR, nearly causing me to drop the phone.

"Tell them she's not breathing." Tears stream down his face as he continues to press on her chest. "TELL THEM." He screams.

I do my best to relay the information, but the intake of breath behind me forces me to turn around. Roland is standing with his mouth open, watching the horrific scene unfold.

"Shit," I murmur. "Roland, go back to your room."

"Mom? Dad?" He blinks, the confusion marring his perfect little face.

"Ma'am," I whimper to the operator—the only connection to the thin thread of reality. "I need to take my little brother into his room. Can you tell the officers the door is unlocked and to come upstairs? My brother has kicked the gun away from them and is still doing CPR on my mom."

"How about you keep me on speaker and leave it on the ground by your brother?"

I nod, even though she can't see me, and press the speaker button before setting the phone on the ground by my brother as he continues to save our mother.

"Come on, buddy." I grip Roland's shoulders and guide him into my room. "Let's wait in here, ok?"

"Are they...*dead*?" Roland crawls onto the bed and draws his knees to his chest.

"I don't know."

But even as I speak the words, I know they are and everything is about to change. When the flashing lights illuminate the dark sky, it's the moment our world becomes irrevocably altered.

I glance at my baby brother and open the bedroom door. "Wait here."

A flurry of activity fills the usually empty corridor as medics assess both of my parents. The white cloth covering my father tells me what I already know—the monster is *dead*.

The medics load my mother's lifeless body onto the stretcher and rush toward the stairs and out the open front door.

I hear the officers talking as I watch the scene. "Can't believe something like this happens, in a *house* like this. I always wondered if it would come to this. As many times as we got welfare checks here and finding nothing... such a shame. Now we know why the rich asshole didn't have a gate or guards. He didn't want anyone seeing who he really was."

They're not wrong. It's exactly why we didn't have any staff and everything was left to my mom or us to do. The comments don't shock me or make me mad, not when they are true. But what I'm not prepared for, I seeing my brother be drug away in handcuffs.

"Hey," I scream, rushing toward him. "Where are you taking him?"

"It's standard procedure, son. In fact—" the surly man nods toward his partner. "They all need to be brought in."

"You're *arresting* him?"

"Drake." Gage's calm voice snaps my attention toward him. "Get Roland. It's going to be okay, but you need to be there for him."

"Gage... what's going to happen now?"

"I don't know, buddy. I don't know."

I fetch Roland from my room and hold his hand in mine as we walk down the stairs with the uniformed man, to his awaiting car. The uniformed officer helps us inside the backseat and closes the door. The metal slamming is like a coffin sealing our fate inside.

"Drake?" Roland looks up at my face. "Who's going to take care of us now? Are they going to take us away?"

"No, buddy. No one is ever going to split us up. Not forever, anyway. Do you hear me? It's us now. You, me, and Gage."

As the car pulls away from our home, I can't silence the voices in my head telling me I just lied to my little brother. My parents were supposed to love us. But for years, all we got was violence and heartbreak. And if that's what *love* does to someone, I wanted nothing to do with it.

From this moment forward, my brothers would be the only people I loved. Because letting someone in meant taking a risk.

And opening yourself up to someone else meant experiencing something I'd rather not... heartbreak.

1

Drake

Twenty years later.

I listen as the judge issues the verdict. The sound of the gavel cracking against the wooden desk gives me a thrill that will leave me on a high for the rest of the day. My client has been fighting for a divorce for nearly a year. I thought the damn thing would never end, but by luck's chance, we caught her now ex-husband with his pants down. *Literally.*

I watch as she gathers her two daughters and hugs them close. For years, she'd been subjected to his mental torture, and when her eldest daughter tried to commit suicide, she knew it was time to get out. And I got to be the sadistic motherfucker to hammer his sorry ass to the floor.

There's something about seeing a man crumble beneath the weight of the law that makes me feel alive. It's like watching filth wash down into the gutter after a hard rain. I hate men like the ones I take to court. They remind me of *him*. The man who destroyed everything in his path until it finally destroyed him—my father.

The sound of traffic on the street tugs me from the memory I've spent years trying to bury in the recesses of my mind. It does me no good to hold on to the past—even though some would tell you I carry the weight of it with me daily.

The only positive thing that came out of my childhood was the money. And even *it* carries a black mark that leaves my mouth sour with revulsion when I think about it.

When we buried my parents twenty years ago, we feared our family—what was left of it—would be split up. Miraculously, my dad's sister stepped in. Until that moment, we'd known very little about her, as she'd been estranged from our father. Me, Gage, and Roland were apprehensive about living with her, but we came to realize pretty quickly she wasn't like our dad. From that day forward, she raised the three of us like her own. Well, mostly just me and Roland.

Gage was seventeen at the time and somehow got into college, despite our family troubles. He stayed local, afraid to leave me and Roland after everything we'd been through. It shocks me how well he did in school, despite the role he had in ending the reign of the man who'd sired us.

Gage is now a successful orthopedic surgeon here in Atlanta. His skills are sought after all over the country, leaving him little time for much else. It doesn't matter, though. We all decided, not long after our parents' deaths, to avoid relation-ships outside the one we have with each other. Love isn't worth the trouble. That mentality earned us the reputation of being casual kings with women—and we don't care.

No attachments mean no heartache.

My phone vibrates inside my pocket as I tug my car door open. Roland's face flashes across the screen, making me smile.

"Roland." I close myself inside my car and press the start button. The phone switches over to Bluetooth, allowing me to toss the phone in my seat. "Where are you? I thought you had a show tonight?"

"I do. I'm headed there now." His raspy voice makes me smile.

Roland found his love for music at an early age. I suspect it was from all the times I'd turned it on to drown out the yelling, but it inevitably led to him breaking the Top 100 Billboard list.

At twenty-four, Roland has amassed his own wealth. He's the lead singer for Savage Realm. His music floats somewhere between pop and rock. His look, however, screams something else entirely. Roland refuses to conform to the typical musician look. With his dirty blonde hair and glasses, he doesn't look like a rock star. Instead, he resembles someone you'd find at a poetry slam on a Wednesday night.

"What's up? Everything okay?" I ask, confused but happy to hear his voice.

"Yeah… I just wanted to tell you I'll be in town in two days. We added a concert in Atlanta, and I wanted to see you guys. What's the chance you'll come to my show?"

He knows Gage and I hate the music scene, but he's my baby brother and I'd die for him. So going to his show isn't a hardship.

"We'll be there. Call my office and give my secretary the details. I'll call Gage and let him know."

"Great. Look, we're about to start setup. I'll call your office tomorrow. Love you, bro."

"Love you, too, Roland. Be safe and knock 'em dead."

I press the button on my steering wheel and speak Gage's name into the car. Court ended earlier than expected and, glancing at the clock, I suspect Gage is between surgeries.

"I take it court went well." Gage's voice filters through the line.

"Yep. That mother fucker had no leg to stand on when we showed the judge the photos of him buried balls deep in his mistress. His days of playing mental warfare on his wife and kids are over. He'll have supervised visitation for the next year."

"You really *are* a dick." Gage laughs heartily through the phone.

"It pays the bills—being a dick, that is."

"What's up? You lucked out and caught me in between surgery. But..." Gage gets quiet for a moment and the sound of him shuffling something in the background echoes in my ear. "I have to head up to talk with the parents."

"Roland is in town in two days. We're going to see him. Clear your schedule."

"At least it's a Saturday. I was supposed to be on call in the ER, but I'll swap with Peterson."

"Good. I'll call you tonight with the details. Go break a leg." I smile as he chuffs another laugh into the phone.

"Fuck you, Drake."

The line goes dead, leaving me with an impish grin that covers my face. I navigate my Dodge Challenger Hellcat through the busy Atlanta streets and pull into the parking garage beneath my building.

I didn't want the drama of renting a space from someone, so I used the blood money left behind by my dad and bought my own. The top two floors are converted into living space, and the remaining twenty are for businesses. My firm takes up floors twelve through sixteen. I lease the remaining fifteen to various organizations that help women and survivors of domestic violence. A family counseling center, relocation services, employment help, temporary housing, private security, and investigations, and my legal team makes up the corporation I call Angel's Wings. A corporation started in honor of my mother.

The attorney portion of the corporation is headed by me, along with three other attorneys who work for me. A criminal defense attorney, real estate attorney, and entertainment attorney. While I could practice law in all four areas, I focus on saving those who can't save themselves.

"Max." I tip my head at my head of security, who's watching me as I enter. "Anything I need to know about?"

"No, sir. All's been quiet." He grins. "Just the way I like it."

"Perfect. You know where to find me if anything changes."

I press the button for the elevator and wait. My mind drifts back to the woman's expression when she heard the judge announce his decision. It was mixed with relief and sadness, but beneath it all, I saw hope.

Something my mother never got.

The ping of the elevator's arrival snaps me from my thoughts, and I step inside. Leaning against the metal wall, I press the illuminated digit for my firm.

The day is young, which means more work is waiting for me. Glancing at my watch, I sigh, seeing its nearing three o'clock.

It's a Thursday, and, like most weekdays, I won't go upstairs until well after night has fallen. Work is all that matters outside my brothers and aunt. Sure... I take care of my carnal needs, but that's just sex. Finding a woman to satisfy those needs takes little effort at the club—plus, I have Kat whenever I need her.

The metal doors open to a silent floor, allowing me to step out unnoticed. Carly, my receptionist, purses her lips as I approach the front desk.

"Mr. Winston." She grinds her teeth together and blows out a frustrated breath. "Mrs. Davidson is waiting in your office."

Carly despises Mrs. Davidson. While most of my cases involve domestic violence, I occasionally take on a rich wife who finds her husband's boredom has led his dick into their nanny. Mrs. Davidson is one of those women, and she is what Carly calls *high maintenance*.

"Was she on my calendar?" I cock an eyebrow, knowing the answer is no—I know my schedule like the back of my hand.

"No. She wasn't. And when I mentioned that tidbit to that wretched woman, she stomped her foot like a twelve-year-old child. She was making a scene, so I sent her in *there* to wait on you."

I roll my eyes in response and grunt. "Great. Look." I start past her, but pause. "Roland will call in the next day with details on his visit. Block out my calendar this weekend and get the details for me if I'm not available to chat with him."

"Of course." She waves her hand through the air, ushering me towards my office. "Have fun. I'm pretty sure her breasts are going to pop out of that thing she's calling a dress. I think she's trying to find her next husband." Carly smirks as I shoot her the bird in response. Carly has worked for me since opening day, and she's more like a distant cousin than an employee.

"Not happening."

I pause outside the door and take a deep breath. My mood has been on a high... but something tells me Mrs. Davidson is about to send it on a nosedive.

I push inside and force a fake grin at the plastic woman sitting in the chair across from my desk. Carly was accurate in saying she was close to popping out of her outfit. The red bodycon dress is obviously two sizes too small and does little to cover her up.

"Mrs. Davidson. Did we have an appointment I forgot about?"

"Hello, Mr. Winston." She purrs, leaning closer to the edge of my desk, causing her boobs to rest against the wooden top. "No. We didn't. But I wanted to come by and see you."

"For what? I don't have any new information and my PI hasn't found anything yet."

She cocks her head and grins. "Let's not pretend." She stands and presses her hands into the top of my desk. "I am tired of being lonely and you're a single guy."

Under my breath, I murmur, "And even *I* have standards." Matching the plastic stiffness of her grin, I reply out loud, "What does that have to do with your case, Mrs. Davidson?"

She shrugs her shoulders shamelessly, obviously intending to squish her breasts together in a way that almost spills them out of the pathetic excuse for clothing. "Nothing."

"Then you should go. I'm not interested in your games, nor will I cross that line with a client. If you're needing someone to fuck—" she gasps at my callous words "—then go out and find a dick willing. Because this—" I wave my hands between us "—will never happen. I don't sleep with clients."

Her face morphs into a mask of rage. She stands straight, pushing both her breasts and chin out as she speaks. "I see. I'm sorry to have disturbed you, Mr. Winston."

"See yourself out. When I have information, I'll call you. Don't show up here unannounced again or I'll find you a new lawyer."

She nods her head as she leaves my office. I enjoy a good fuck. But sleeping with clients is not something I do. I have very specific ways to let my inner demons out—and a client isn't it. I'll never cross that line.

Not now. Not *ever*.

I open my laptop and get to work on one of my other cases. This is what I live for. Nothing and nobody will ever destroy what I've built.

My empire is locked down like Fort Knox—just like my heart.

There isn't a soul that can change that.

2

Drake

THE RHYTHMIC SOUND of bass shakes the walls of the room. Deep burgundy of the walls surrounding me holds a seductive glow from the dimmed lights overhead. My eyes scan the room of guests as I sip the amber liquid from my glass. It's been weeks since I've stepped inside these walls, but after Mrs. Davidson threw herself at me, I was reminded how long it's been since I've had a sexual encounter. And I realized this was long overdue.

I've sworn off relationships, but not fucking. I'm too damaged for a serious relationship... the chances of becoming like my father are too high, and I won't do that to a woman. Not after watching the life drain from my mother's eyes. She'd died long before the monster, whose blood runs through my veins, killed her. This is the only way I feel safe... feel—in control.

It's the only way I can keep the monster buried deep, only letting him out to play when I allow it. No woman would want me if she knew the depravity I need to stay in control.

I down the remaining contents of my glass and set it aside. The person I've been waiting for has finally arrived. I know it's her despite the mask covering her face—her fiery red hair stands out among the others. She's the only woman who can handle what I dish out. I'm certain her demons rival mine, but we've never spoken about the outside world. I'm not even sure the name she's given me is her real one. But that won't stop me from taking her to a private room.

"You're here." Her blood-red nails trail down the white button-up shirt I have on, eliciting goosebumps to erupt across my skin.

I grab her wrist, halting her wandering fingers, and pull her flush against me. "I've been busy." She smiles at my words. Her lip catches between her teeth as she looks up and flutters her eyelashes at me. "Are you ready to obey me, *pet*?"

She hisses, her core grinding against my knee, and I can feel the heat of her pussy through my slacks, making my cock jump in anticipation.

"Yes, sir."

I drop her arm and start toward the hallway that leads to the playrooms.

I don't need to tell her to follow me. She already knows the rules. The minute we step into our roles... I become her master. Anything I demand, she complies and does. It's what I need... what I *crave*.

I step into the room and close the door behind us. "Kneel." I step around her, slowly undoing the buttons of my shirt. "What shall we do tonight?" I speak out loud, mostly to myself. She doesn't get a say in what I choose. The only power she has is her safe word—which she rarely uses. Kat, the name I call her by, enjoys the pain as much as I get off on providing it for her. The first night I met her, I nearly came in my boxers just watching her orgasm from the twisted way I touched her.

My fingers search the drawers until they find what I want. Each of the private rooms is stocked with all the toys one might need in a private session. Besides the tools at my disposal, a massive bed and a Saint Andrew's cross fill the room.

"Stand up." I bark at her. Kat complies immediately, moving from her knees to her feet instantly. "Strip. I need you completely naked."

I watch as she peels the corset off her body. She reaches for the thigh highs to remove them, but I stop her. "Leave them on and get on the bed."

Kat scrambles to the center of the bed and waits for my order. I walk to the edge and run my hand down the side of her face. My fingers trace her collarbone, pausing at her full breasts. Kat has large boobs, which are definitely fake. It's a turn off for me, but the rest of what she offers makes up for it. I circle her erect nipple with the pad of my thumb before pinching it between my fingers. Her eyes close in response to the painful stimulation the pressure I'm applying gives her. She learned a long time ago, making any kind of unsolicited noise results in punishment. Sometimes she defies me just to earn a paddle across her ass—but not tonight. Tonight, she needs exactly what I came to give her.

"Take my cock out." I order her, needing some of my pain eased while I continue to play.

Kat keeps her eyes down as she flicks the button to my jeans open and pushes them down past my hips.

"Just remember, you're not allowed to come." I murmur, my tone edged with hate, the innate desire to torment her making my cock harden with delight. "Grab my dick and jack me off." I bark out. My desire is uncontrollable—almost feral.

Kat wraps her palm around my shaft and pauses. "May I get you wet, sir?" Her voice is breathy as she continues to put on the show. She knows it's the only way to push me anywhere near the release I so desperately need.

"Yes." I hiss as her head bows and her lips encase my tip. My balls throb with pleasure as she bobs against my shaft. My fingers wind into her hair. I shove her down on my steel rod, making her take me all the way to the back of her throat. I push without regard for her wellbeing until she's gagging when my crown hits the back. I hold her there ruthlessly as I feel her struggle, chuckling with delight. "That's it. Fuck my dick with your throat, little whore."

The tingling in my spine tells me I'm about to come. I yank against the tresses of her hair, jerking her off my cock. I'm not ready to spill my load just yet, and I didn't plan to do it this way tonight. I tug her hair, using it to guide her to the bench that sits at the foot of the bed. Pushing her forward, I bend her over the edge, which puts her ass on perfect display.

"Don't move." I slap my palm across her flesh, leaving a perfect imprint of my hand. Once more, I return to the dresser and pull out another toy. This one benefits us both when I stick my cock inside her. Kat stays perfectly still as I move around the room and position myself behind her again once more.

She hisses at the sensation of cool liquid dripping along her crevice as I coat her backside in lube. Once I have her sufficiently coated in the slick gel, I squeeze the globes of her ass.

Without bothering to ask for her permission, I press the butt plug into her ass and pop her hard. She cries out and tenses, the apology spilling out of her mouth just like I've programmed her to do. "I'm sorry, Sir."

"It's all right, pet. Your scream makes my dick harder." I smooth my hand across her flesh and pop her again. "My cock needs to be buried inside your tight cunt."

Kat whimpers her reply, no doubt anticipating what she knows is coming next. I grab the condom I'd laid on the bed earlier and sheath myself in the barrier. I've never fucked a woman without protection, and I don't plan to. Knocking someone up is my idea of a death sentence. Kids are something I *never* want, especially not with some faceless receptacle who is here only for my pleasure.

I wouldn't bring a child into the world, knowing I could turn out like my father. Lost in the memory of my past, I ram myself into her awaiting center. Kat cries out with the force of my thrust, her body jolting forward and nearly toppling off the bench. My hands shoot out, steadying her in place as I pump my hips into her, the bench underneath her scraping against the floor.

My thumb presses into the plastic adorning her tight ring, as my cock pushes in and out of her dripping center. Kat moans, unable to bite back the sound escaping her lips. I slap her ass cheek with each escaped sound as I continue to drive into her. The sensation of the butt plug pressing against my shaft is pure bliss, but I need more. I need to dominate her—to *own* her.

My cock springs free, and I pull out and grab her off the bench. I shove her against the Saint Andrew's cross and press her palms against the wooden arms. Latching her wrists in the leather cuffs, I reach between us, fisting my shaft as I kick her feet apart. This is the side of me I could never show to someone outside of these walls. This is the part of me I blame on my father—the torment and depravity I need to inflict on someone makes me a monster. Sex is the only way I can control the need to dominate women. My fingers wrap around her neck, squeezing into her flesh as I bark my orders at her, "Wrap your ankles behind me."

Kat locks her ankles behind me, suspending her body from the floor. Her moans fill the room as I drive myself inside her, fucking her without regard for the stress this position puts on her arms that are hanging off the cross. The friction sends sparks of fire through my veins, making me increase my punishment to her pussy. My balls smack against her as I drive into her, demanding the screams she's belting into the room. I want them—*need* them, knowing it will push me to the release that's close to the edge already.

Kat cries out as her walls tighten around my shaft and pulse. Fire starts at the base of my spine and burns a trail of hot molten lava straight to my shaft. I groan as the warm liquid spurts out of my shaft, filling the condom inside her. Kat's legs drop to the floor as I yank free of her body. I release her hands, still pinned against the wooden cross, holding her upright.

Undoing the buckles, Kat drops to the floor. I take several deep breaths to center myself before barking my next command at her. "Clean me off." I watch as Kat turns toward me and rolls the used condom from my shaft. She ties it off and tosses it in a nearby trashcan before taking her place before me. Holding my gaze, she leans forward and licks the remnants of our coupling from my dick. As she hollows out her cheeks around my length and I feel myself start to harden again, I reach down and press the heel of my hand against her forehead with a shake of my head, knowing she's trying to stretch this out. Her shoulders immediately deflate as she sits back on her heels, adjusting the mask still clinging to her face with a pouty frown on her lips - the only thing I allow to be exposed.

Turning away, I shake my head as I mutter, "I'm going to get cleaned up. See yourself out."

I stalk from the bed and walk into the attached private bathroom. Kat knows the rules. When I'm done, she needs to disappear before I emerge from the shower. This is only sex, and any lingering on her part means we'd never meet up again. No attachments are allowed. And even though she and I hook up often—it's nothing more than a Dom and his sub. If she gets any other ideas in her head, I'll replace her fast.

Just as I expect, Kat is gone when I finally emerge from the shower. She tidied up the room and laid my clothing on the bed. After pulling on my clothes, I tug my phone from my pants pocket. I find the person I want in my contacts and press the phone to my ear.

"What's up?" His gruff voice fills the line.

"Meet me at my house for a drink." I smile, knowing he won't refuse.

"Fine. I'm just getting off, so give me a few to change my clothes."

"I'm just leaving the club, anyway. I'll meet you at my place."

"The club, huh? Find anyone worthwhile?"

Much like me, my brothers have fallen into the lifestyle as well. It's a safe release for the polluted blood our dad graced us with. We find being a Dominant gives us the control we need without actually hurting anyone. The thought of losing control like we witnessed so many times as a kid scares the shit out of us. Being a Dom in the club keeps *us* sane and women safe. We agreed years ago to steer clear of long-term commitments. Not knowing what our future would be, it's our way of protecting innocent women. That, and the careers we each have chosen as adults.

Navigating my car onto the road, I inhale a deep breath and sigh. I long for a normal life, but it's just a fantasy I know I'll never have. I'm better off alone... even if I *am* lonely. Monsters belong in the dark.

3

Drake

ALL I CAN HEAR through the ramblings of the defense attorney is my client's quiet sniffles. It's like a dagger to my soul, knowing she's reliving the awful memories of being married to the douche bag currently smirking in our direction. It's sad watching him sit there on his high horse, not knowing what's about to happen. His schmuck of an attorney actually thinks he's winning this case. I struggle not to laugh out loud. Truly. My patience is long gone.

I steal another glance at the woman who endured enough torment to earn her a solid place in heaven and give her a knowing nod. As soon as the opposing counsel is done spewing his lies, I stand and unbutton my jacket. The chair makes a scraping sound across the hardwood floors of the courtroom, causing her soon to be ex-husband to glance my direction.

"Your Honor." I speak, my voice calm as I move around the table separating me from his bench. "I'd like to present these items as evidence, if I may."

"Wait." The sleazy-looking attorney cries out. "This wasn't made available in the disclosure of documents."

"Correct. This evidence didn't exist during that phase of discovery. It was actually just discovered, but I assure you it's quite relevant to the case. It has everything to do with the defendant's character. I'd like to enter these items in as exhibit b." I pass over copies to the opposing counsel and stride to the judge to hand him the documents. I can't help the satisfying smirk I shoot at his client, knowing nothing he can say will dig him out of the mess he's made for himself. "As you can see, your Honor," I turn and face the courtroom, which is mostly empty except for my client's parents and the social worker assigned to the case. "Mr. Hargrove was, in fact, having an affair. Multiple affairs, if we're being honest, which, I'd like to remind the court, is the entire purpose of being here. We just couldn't *prove* his lies until now."

"Objection." His attorney, Jack Prince, blurts out. His face red as he approaches the judge, scrambling to salvage his case. "We were not made aware of any new evidence in this case. This information should not be allowed."

"Overruled." The judge's gavel strikes the wooden surface, silencing the anxious chatter in the courtroom. "Mr. Hargrove...." He slides his glasses down his nose and peers out over his desk as the vein along the side of his forehead bulges. "...it would appear this is you in several of the photos presented here — and I do not see Mrs. Hargrove in any of them. Counsel, I'm going to need a short recess to go over these documents and photos to assess them for validity and pertinence to this case. Let's take a quick break and return here in one hour." He slams the tiny mallet on the table and dismisses us.

I knew this would be a possibility. The judge overseeing this divorce is a by-the-book man, especially when children are involved. Calista Hargrove sought me out over a year ago when she found evidence her husband was cheating on her. When she confronted him about it, Kent Hargrove lost his mind. It was the first time Calista had seen the physically abusive side of her husband. Until then, he'd only been verbally and mentally abusive. When Calista told him she was leaving, Kent threatened to take the kids. Even though Calista was the one who had tended to their two small children while he worked and fucked around, Kent scared her into staying. Typical two-faced abuser. Until she found him in their bed with the nineteen-year-old nanny. A nanny that she didn't want *or* need.

Instead of telling him to get out, she walked out of the bedroom and pretended it didn't happen. But what Kent didn't know was Calista came to my building seeking help in getting out of the hellish marriage. For the last year, we had him followed. It took time for the asshole to screw up, but my private investigator got the evidence we need to end this sham of a union and set her and her two girls free.

"What does this mean?" Calista's small voice whispers behind me.

My eyes find her standing beside her father, who looks equally concerned. He still beats himself up every day over their marriage, saying he should have known something was wrong. It's going to take him some time to come to grips with the fact that Kent Hargrove is good at fooling the people around him, and nothing he could have done would change the course of how this is all playing out. It always takes time. Monsters walk around in broad daylight because they wear masks of innocence to fool their victims until it's too late.

That is why I do what I do—to save the ones I can in *her* name. The one who couldn't escape.

"It doesn't mean a thing. It's simply a formality with the judge. He's a stickler for following the rules and if I know him, he's in his chambers sifting through the documents and photos. This is good, Calista. By tonight, you'll be a free woman. You and your beautiful girls will be set for life and can start over anywhere you want."

"I'm moving back home with my parents. I want my girls to grow up where I did—and feel safe."

"That's probably a good plan. Make sure you give my staff your forwarding address so I can put you in touch with resources. The girls might be young, but they'll need counseling. Don't think otherwise. You, too. You've dealt with a lot these past eighteen months." I know from personal experience how therapy can help. Roland and I both attended sessions for the first year after my parent's death. Our aunt insisted upon it.

I usher them to grab lunch and remind them to return in forty-five minutes. We don't want to be late for the judge. He loathes tardiness in his courtroom and while I'm confident this case will soon be closed... I don't want to rock the boat. I make my way down to the café on the bottom floor of the courthouse, not wanting to stray too far.

As I step off the elevator, my phone buzzes in my pocket. I'm not at all surprised to see Gage's face illuminating the screen.

"What's up, big brother?"

"You in court?" His voice sounds strained.

"Nope. Something wrong?" My hackles rise, making the hairs on the back of my neck stand.

"Kind of. Look, I had a woman come into the ER with a broken collarbone and right wrist. She claims it was from slipping on spilled water, but..." His voice trails off. I can tell in his tone he doesn't think she's telling the truth.

"You think it's domestic violence?"

"I do. But when I pressed the matter, she clammed up and wouldn't answer any more questions." He sighs into the phone. It isn't like Gage to take interest in his patients beyond their visits to the ER or operating room. "Then her husband showed up and I couldn't press anymore."

"You want me to do some digging?"

"Not yet. But I'm going to send you her information. Will you just keep an ear to the ground? Let me know if you hear something?"

"Yeah. Gage?" I furrow my brow and pinch the bridge of my nose. "Is there something I need to know about this woman? Do you know her or something?"

He grumbles something unintelligible into the phone and huffs. "Or something. Look, I've got to go. A crash victim is coming in and they need me. I'll text you the info."

"Alright. Don't forget tomorrow. I'll meet you at your place at five."

"That's right. We're going to see Roland's band." Gage groans. "Gotta go. See you then."

My phone vibrates in my palm as I pull it from my face. Gage is possibly violating patient confidentiality in so many ways by sending me the information, but if it bothers him enough to risk it, I'll do what I can to help him.

"You think you're the shit, don't you?" The disgruntled voice of Kent Hargrove has me glancing over my shoulder.

"Mr. Hargrove." I resume filling the Styrofoam cup in my hand, not paying any mind to his snide comment.

"I'm talking to you." He grunts louder.

"I heard you. But I'm choosing to ignore you. It'd do you well to stop talking and find your attorney."

"Fuck you." He steps in front of me, blocking my path to the exit. "You think you can just ruin people's lives and get away with it?"

"Mr. Hargrove. I'm going to assume your anger is what's causing you to say stupid things to me. Otherwise, the threat you're making right now will land you in jail. Now—" I step around him. "I'll see you back in the courtroom."

"You think this is done?"

His depraved laugh causes me to spin on my heel and grip the front of his shirt. My coffee splashes over the rim, dotting his crisp white shirt with scolding hot liquid. His grimace is subtle, but he quickly schools his expression. I would have missed it if I hadn't been paying attention to him. I'm not about to let the little shit threaten anymore people. The courtroom isn't the only place I'm known as a coldhearted bastard.

"Listen, you sniveling fuck." I tighten my grip on the cheap fabric of his button down. "You may intimidate women with this pussy bullshit, but *I'm* not afraid of you. And I'm certainly not afraid to stomp your worthless ass outside of that courtroom, too. Now I'll say it again." I let him go and step back. "Find your attorney and keep your mouth shut. Or your wallet won't be the only thing hurting."

The café is dead silent throughout our exchange. The only sound is the thumping of his heart beating wildly against his ribs, as his eyes dilate with my threat. I straighten my jacket and step back, putting much-needed space between us. Kent Hargrove's chest pumps with the fury he's desperately trying to contain. I want to laugh at his stupidity. Instead, I drain the cup, then crumple the remnants of my coffee and toss it into the receptacle bin beside him.

"See you in the courtroom, Mr. Hargrove."

By the time I arrive on the third floor, I'm more primed than ever to demolish the asshole. Kent is the worst kind of man. He controls women with intimidation and threats. It's the only way men like him can compensate for their own insecurities. And the problem with that mentality is the collateral damage is usually someone who can't stand up for themselves.

Calista Hargrove steps up to the table beside me and slides into the vacant chair. I pull the chair next to her out and sit down. Still reeling over her soon to be ex's behavior in the café, I take a calming breath to soothe the pulsing vein in my head.

"Everything okay?" Calista leans close and whispers.

"Yes. Had an interesting conversation with Mr. Douchenugget at lunch."

"Oh, God." She gasps. "Is something wrong?"

"No. But I will be making a change to the settlement request."

Her face blanches at my words. But I simply hold my finger up. "Trust me."

She takes a deep breath and nods. We watch as Kent and his attorney stroll into the courtroom and take their seats. The judge enters, forcing us all to stand until he is seated.

"I've reviewed the documents and have to say." He takes his glasses off before continuing. "Mr. Hargrove, you've surprised me, and I've been doing this for a long time. You had to know you would be watched like a hawk, yet you not only continued your sordid affairs... you flaunted them. And with girls—not women. I've asked the district attorney's office to look into the information because I want to be certain the young ladies you were filmed with were of legal age. Some of them are rather questionable. I'm not only granting the restraining order for Ms. Hargrove, but I'm strongly recommending supervised visitation—indefinitely. Those images will haunt me for years to come. Your beautiful daughters do not deserve that stain on their young lives." The judge shakes his head. "Does the plaintiff have any further requests?"

"We do, your honor." I stand and rap my knuckles across the wooden table. "In light of the newest evidence, I would like to amend the monetary portion of our claim. Besides child support and alimony, we would like the current shared residences sold and then have the profits placed into a trust fund for the girls' education. One that Mr. Kent can't distribute funds from..."

"Your Honor." Jack Prince, opposing counsel, interjects. "The house has already been included in the agreement. My client has agreed to sell their home."

"I'm not talking about the couple's residence." I cock an eyebrow at him, waiting for the realization to settle in.

"Fuck." Mr. Hargrove explodes beside Jack. "*No*."

"Kent." His attorney waves his hand. "Settle down."

"What is this about?" The judge hammers the gavel in front of him. "Both of you. Step forward."

I hammer the final nail into the coffin and meet Jack at the desk. "This shows three more properties owned by Mr. Hargrove. He thought putting them in his mistress's names would keep them out of this case, but as usual, my investigator found them. We'd like these liquidated and put into a trust for his daughters."

The judge reads over the information and grunts. "Your client is a real piece of work, Mr. Prince. I'll be adding this to the settlement. Now, back to your tables."

Jack grumbles as he moves to stand beside Mr. Hargrove. My smug expression makes him stew with anger as I take my spot back at ours. Calista stands beside me, waiting for the judge's final word.

"I've seen a lot of crazy stuff in my time as a judge. But Mr. Hargrove… this might take the cake. You threw your perfect family aside to indulge in something that very well might land you in jail. Time will tell on that front. In the meantime, I'm granting Ms. Hargrove's petition for divorce. She will retain full custody of the two minor children. You will pay child support in the agreed amount in the final document, as well as liquidate all properties owned. The proceeds from the sale of said properties will be placed in a trust fund for the girls, to be managed by their mother, Calista Hargrove. I am also extending the restraining order for life. You will be able to visit the girls, but only in the presence of an appointed social worker. Mr. Hargrove…" The judge clears his throat. "Men like you disgust me. If I ever see you in my court again, I won't be so lenient. Ms. Hargrove." He turns to us and gives her a sympathetic smile. "This is your chance to reinvent yourself. The world is your oyster, so grab hold and make it good. And do me a favor?"

"Yes, sir?" Her voice cracks with emotion as her fingers dig into the desk for stability.

"Pick better your next go round and don't settle for shit like him."

"I will. Thank you, your Honor."

"This court is adjourned."

The sound of his gavel hitting the desktop is like the slot machine spitting out an epic jackpot of winnings. I shove all the papers scattered on the table in front of me into my leather briefcase. I turn toward my client, who's wrapped up in her parents' embrace, spilling over with emotion. It's a sight that makes my chest tighten with unresolved feelings of my own. I never had that kind of relationship with my parents. My mom was too wrapped up in trying to keep my dad happy when he was home, and my dad—well, he was an asshole. The only thing I have to thank him for is my epic drive to slaughter men like him.

"Thank you." Calista turns and embraces me in a hug.

Her arms wrap around my midsection, making me stiffen at the sensation. Physical touch isn't something I've ever sought from women. I've come to accept the women I help in court will show this type of gratitude, but it doesn't make me react with sunshine and butterflies.

"You're welcome. But do me a favor." Calista steps back and smiles as I speak. "Don't forget to leave your new address and contact information with my receptionist. I'm serious about making sure you get help wherever you settle."

"How is it you're still single?" She tilts her head at me, her eyes full of genuine curiosity. "You're a good man, Mr. Winston."

"Marriage isn't in the cards for me, Calista. I'm not wired for that. It's a rule I've lived by my whole life and I'm content with that."

"I think you're mistaken. One day, you'll meet a woman who will knock you on your ass and make you forget your silly rule. I don't know how I'll ever thank you."

"The nice sized check your douche of an ex has to write me is thanks enough. But really... make a good life for those two girls of yours and that's all the thanks I need. Now. Go. Get your daughters and start your life."

I walk them out of the courtroom and ride the elevator down to the exit with them. It makes me feel good to watch her walk out with her parents, knowing they will help her build a better life. I wait until they're out of sight and make my way over to the parking garage. Court might be over for the Hargrove's, but I have a pile of files waiting for me back at the office. I fist my key fob in my pocket and click the button to unlock the door. The crisp leather smell wafts out as I slide in behind the steering wheel. I can't help but replay Calista's words in my head.

One day, you'll meet a woman who will knock you on your ass and make you forget your silly rule.

She's wrong. No woman will ever make me forget the promise I made years ago. I won't risk it. My dad's blood runs through my veins, and that means I could turn into the same monster he was. Besides... there's no woman strong enough to deal with my needs outside the club. That is the reason I keep things purely sexual with women. I don't date and rarely hook up. I've learned even hook-ups can get messy. And messy isn't my thing.

I shift my car into reverse and pull out of the garage. This is the life I'm destined to live. My brothers and I agreed that bringing a partner into the fray would only barter trouble in the long run. My mind drifts to Roland. It's been a while since Gage and I have seen him. This weekend is long overdue. Getting the gang back together.

The three of us are all we've ever had… and it is enough.

4

Drake

GAGE IS comical as we amble up the walkway toward the back entrance. Roland couriered backstage passes to my office yesterday. This isn't a new rodeo for us. Every time we come to one of his concerts, we enter through the employee doors. His security staff knows us—but sometimes the venue staff fucks with us.

Tonight… is no exception.

Security staff at the Mercedes Benz stadium are a bunch of uneducated, wannabe cops who get off on hassling any-and-everyone. Typically, Gage and I dress like the billionaires we worked our asses off to become, but we opted for a more casual look tonight. Going to a concert in an Armani suit seemed like overkill. I guess that's why the moron standing guard at the employee entrance thinks it's wise to shake us down. Gage is ready to explode on the idiot and just about does, but Roland pops out at the right moment. I texted him to tell him we were being detained and might not make it in to see him before he went on stage—which led to the current situation.

"What's your name?" Roland stands a foot from the polo-wearing guard. His arms are folded across his chest, and anyone can see he is fuming mad.

"Patrick, sir." The young kid's—yes, kid—voice wavers under my brother's scrutinizing gaze.

"Do you realize you might single-handedly be the reason my show is delayed?"

"I was just doing my job." He takes a deep breath and rolls his eyes at the sky. "I swear I wasn't trying to be a dick."

"Your job. Right. And did you notice their passes to be back here? Or were you more concerned with waving your tiny dick around pretending to be a cop? Because to me that's what this looks like." Roland waves us through the door and grunts. "You're done for the day, son. Run home to mommy and tell her how she fucked up raising you. Come on, bros. I don't have a lot of time to catch up thanks to this… shoulda been a cum stain."

Gage shakes his head as we follow Roland up the stairs that lead to his dressing room. Roland is thirteen years younger than Gage—which usually means Gage has no idea what Roland is saying half the time. Not that he and I are really any closer in age. At thirty-two, I'm still a decade older than him, leaving me scratching my own head at most of his antics as well.

"I've missed you, little brother." I tug him into a hug as soon as we're inside the room. "How the hell have you been?"

"Good. The tour is almost done, so I'll be home in a few months." Roland plops down on the leather couch and rests his feet on the glass table. "I'm ready for a break, though."

"A break?" I share a confused glance with Gage. We've never heard Roland say he wants or needs a break.

"Is something wrong?" Gage raises a brow in question. "You've never taken a break."

Roland leans his head back and blows out an exaggerated breath. "I know. But I'm exhausted. I want to slow down and maybe write some new music. I've been moving non-stop for the last eighteen months and just need—"

"Rest?" I finish for him. "I get it. You deserve to stop and enjoy the fruits of your hard work, Rol. No need to explain."

"Mr. Winston." A feminine voice had us all turning toward the door. "They're asking for you backstage."

"Right." Roland stands and pops his neck. "Tell them I'll be right up, Isabella."

"Isabella?" Gage scrunches his face.

"She's my public relations specialist. The label seemed to think I needed help with my image. They hired her a few months ago." A myriad of emotion scatters across his face but are gone almost as quickly.

"Your *image*? What the fuck does that mean?" I growl in irritation.

I get my brother has done some questionable things, but a public relations specialist? He's twenty-four years old and has more ambition than most kids his age. It's expected that he'd be in the tabloids for partying hard and being with a lot of women based on the lifestyle he leads.

"Apparently being filmed with various women is sending my fans the wrong message. Whatever. She just keeps the media at bay. No big deal."

"If you say so, little brother. But from the sound out there—" Gage points his finger toward the hallway. "—your fans seem to love you just the same."

Roland cuts his eyes toward us with a knowing look. "I gotta go. If she comes back in here, she'll bust my balls for sure. And despite the tabloids' wild opinions of me, that is *not* something I'd enjoy."

Roland hugs us before striding out into the corridor. We get to watch from backstage. Me and Gage hate the massive crowds that turn out for his music. And based on the roaring sounds coming from beyond the stage, the house is packed..

"Why the fuck would he need someone to help him with his image?" Gage grumbles as he leans against the wall. "He hasn't been in the tabloids since last year—after that incident with the supermodel. I had no idea he had a public relations specialist. It's not like he's caught every other weekend with his dick out."

"Honestly I'm not surprised they hired her. I told Roland eventually he would need to chill out. Maybe this will force him to focus on his music and stay out of the media's eye a bit."

I watch with admiration as my younger brother runs out onto the stage. The crowd goes nuts when he grabs the microphone and screams his welcome. Roland has charisma that seems to bleed out of his pores when he's in front of his fans.

"*Welcome Atlanta.*" His voice echoes through the speakers. "*Tonight is going to be fucking amazing. Are you ready?*" he bellows out, revving up the onlookers.

The first chords of his current hit plays. Even though I'm not a fan of this genre of music, I have to admit his newest number one hit *is* one of my favorites.

Hearing him sing the words always gives me chills. Even though he swore it was just lyrics, I truly believe there's a hidden meaning behind it. While Roland had only been four when the shit went down with our parents—he closed himself off to love like Gage and I had. Well… romantic love. We loved each other, and, of course, we cared for our aunt. Had it not been for her, we would have ended up in the system. Listening to him move from one song to the next makes me more and more proud with each passing minute.

"Fuck." Gage withdraws his cell phone and steps away with it pressed to his face.

His work never stops. Being good at his job has a price—it means he's always on call. If his body language has anything to say, I can tell the call isn't a pleasant one.

"Everything alright?"

Gage jams the phone into his back pocket and runs his fingers through his hair. "No. I have to go."

"What? *Now?*"

"Apparently there's a judge in the waiting room demanding I come and see to his wife. The hospital board has requested my presence." Gage sighs heavily. The guilt of having to cut the visit short weighs on him.

"Let's tell Roland we're leaving."

"You can stay. I'll just grab an Uber." Gage shakes his head at me.

"Not a chance. If a judge is expecting you to drop your life and come in, I'm going with you. I want to make sure there isn't any unscrupulous intent behind this demand."

Roland wraps up his song and promises to be back after a brief intermission. He tells the crowd that nature calls, and he needs to take care of business—which makes the stadium erupt into laughter.

"Whatdidya think?" Roland pops the lid to a water bottle and chugs its contents.

"Fantastic, as usual. Look." Gage presses his palm against Roland's shoulder. "I have to go. The hospital board called and demanded I come for a VIP patient."

"Really? Who is it? The King of Persia?" Roland chuckles.

"No, a local judge. And he's making a scene in the ER."

"You're going with him, right?" Roland turns toward me, concern glinting in the brilliant blue eyes looking at me.

"Of course. This request reeks of desperation and unscrupulousness." I confirm, knowing Roland wouldn't expect anything less.

"Good. Call me when you're done. Maybe you can meet up with me for a drink. I don't leave until tomorrow. Last stop is Austin, then home for a few months."

"Will do, little bro. Good show. I don't think your fans have lost their liking to you yet." I pat his back. We're interrupted by the PR girl as she steps beside him.

"Roland."

"Isabella." Roland's voice takes on a weird tone, making me shoot him a confused look. "These are my brothers, Gage, and Drake." He motions to us.

"Um. Hi. I go by Izzy, though. Roland talks a lot about you." Isabella shoots him a bitchy stare as she turns her attention back to him. "Can we talk for a moment?"

Roland instantly tenses. His face pales at her request. *"Now?"* His voice is laden with aggravation.

"Please?" She presses her hand to his forearm, making him jerk away.

"You good?" I glance between him and Isabella.

"Yeah. Let me know how it goes."

We watch as he turns and slowly follows Isabella toward his dressing room.

"What the hell was that about?" Gage grumbles.

"I don't know, but I plan to find out. Let's go see what this judge wants so we can meet up with him later. Something is going on with him."

Gage nods in agreement. We have security escort us out and head toward my car. Gage lets out a massive breath as soon as he settles in the passenger seat.

"You good?"

"Yeah. Just tired of the board jerking me around at the hospital."

"Why don't you start a private practice? It isn't like you don't have the money. Hell—I'd back you if you needed more."

"I wouldn't be able to help people in the same way, Drake." Gage leans back on the headrest and closes his eyes.

I know what he means. Being in a hospital and working in the ER gives him the chance to save people who normally wouldn't ask for help. Much of my clientele comes from his referrals. Anytime he comes across a woman or man that was a victim of abuse, he slips them information on Angel's Wings. Two out of three people end up contacting them, seeking help out of their situation. Opening a private practice would mean giving up that part of who he is—the fixer. Being a doctor is Gage's way of atoning for our parents' deaths. Even twenty years later, he still blames himself.

It takes no time getting to the hospital. I park in the emergency room lot, and Gage and I climb out and hurry inside through the ER entrance.

"Dr. Winston." One of the nurses runs toward us. "Thank God you came."

"Are you ok?" Gage grips her forearm as he glances her over.

"Yes, but the—" Her words are interrupted as an older looking man approaches us from the patient area.

"Dr. Winston, it's about fucking time you got here."

"As I was saying—" The nurse shoots him an eat shit look and continues. "Judge Carmichael is here with his wife. She took a nasty spill down the stairs and injured her arm. He demanded that you be the one to assess her."

Judge Carmichael gives me a disgusted look. He and I know each other from interactions in court. Of all the judges I've worked with, I hate him the most. Heath Carmichael is the type of man that makes winning a divorce case difficult. More often than not, he sides with the husband in the case. Several attorneys have complained about his ineptness behind the bench.

"Fine. Take me to her. Drake," Gage turns toward me. "Come back and you can wait at the nurses' station. After you, your

Honor." Gage waves the judge through the double doors.

We head down a series of hallways before the nurse comes to a stop. "This is her room. I can show your brother where to wait. "

Gage nods and waits for the judge to step through the door. As soon as it opens, I get a clear view inside. I'm not prepared for the sight I see. A woman, considerably younger then Heath Carmichael, lies on the hospital bed. From the brief glimpse I get of her, I can see bruising along her hairline, coupled with a slight gash. Her arm is cradled in some kind of splint, obviously waiting for Gage to look it over. She seems to flinch when her husband steps beside her. Something stirs in my chest, making my protective nature rise to the surface. Just as Gage closes the door, she looks up and catches me staring.

Her eyes look vacant and hollow, missing the light I imagine they used to hold. Caught In the trance, I can't tear my gaze from hers. She breaks the connection when she turns her head and a tear trickles down her cheek, spilling onto the crisp white sheet of her bed.

"Mr. Winston?" The nurse whispers, tearing my sights from the judge's wife. "Follow me, please."

I nod, casting one last glance at the now-closed door. Something feels off about the whole situation. It leaves me feeling unsettled. Fell down the stairs? Something tells me *that's* the furthest thing from the truth. I've seen it enough times in my career, and I bet my life if stairs were involved, his wife didn't take the spill down them by accident.

All I can do is hope Gage will dig and get her the resources she needs to get out if she's being hurt.

5

Drake

THE JUDGE STEPS OUT while on his cell phone. From my vantage point, I once again have a clear line of sight into the room. I watch as Gage speaks animatedly to the woman as he speaks freely for the first time since he stepped in there. She still looks to be crying, no doubt from the pain she's in. Her injuries are far from superficial.

"Drake Winston." Judge Carmichael's flat tone breaks my appraisal of his wife.

My eyes trail his body and settle on his piercing glare. "Judge. Sorry about your wife. Hope everything works out okay for her."

He clears his throat. "I'm just glad it didn't turn out worse. She scared me when I saw her trip at the top of the stairs."

"Tripped, huh?" I purse my lips, fighting back the urge to call him out on his bullshit. "Guess it's a good thing you were home to save her."

He ignores the sarcasm in my voice as he titters on, "I'm just glad her arm won't require surgery after all. Your brother is the best and if he says it'll heal on its own—I have to believe him. Surgery would have been *such* an inconvenience."

"Inconvenience?" I let one eyebrow raise slowly as I glance back at the room and catch her watching our interaction.

"Of course. The big charity gala for the hospital is coming up. I'd have hated to miss that—I'm sure Gage's department would miss my, ahem, rather large annual donation."

Of *course*, his tantrum earlier was about money. Judge Carmichael comes from wealth. Not as much as my brothers and I, but money all the same. The difference is his money *buys* people. Mine saves them. Heath Carmichael is nothing but a pretentious prick.

"Will you be attending the gala this year?" His question is filled with the hint of insinuation—of what, I don't know.

"Just like *every* year." I smart off at his asinine question. He knows our involvement with that charity. His question is *meant* to touch a nerve. "I always donate to the hospital. Gage does as well. As you know, money is no object when it's for a cause such as the one coming up."

The hospital's annual charity ball is to raise money for their pro-bono medical cases. They believe in giving back to the community, and this is how they do it. People who need surgery or treatment for whatever ailments they may have, get what they need because the hospital uses the funds raised from the Gala to cover the cost.

"Right. Of course. I forgot your pockets are deeper than mine. Calvin Winston *was* your father, after all."

Just hearing that name makes me bristle with disgust. Heath Carmichael ran in the same circles our father did—they were probably even friends when they were younger. And *that* thought makes me question his character even more.

"Judge." Gage joins us at the nurses' station. "Your wife should be good to go in a couple of hours. I need to get another x-ray before putting her in a cast. I also want to get a head CT to make sure there aren't any complications from hitting her head. She has a pretty nasty bump and a few bruises, but I think that's all. She's very lucky she didn't break her neck."

"Good—good." He pushes his shoulders back and stands taller. "Will Rhiannon be okay to attend the gala next weekend?"

Hearing her name makes me glance back into the room. She's still watching the three of us closely. I smile at her, tipping my head ever so slightly. The gesture causes her to cut her eyes away, in what I assume is embarrassment.

"She should be. That depends on the CT scan. If it shows any abnormalities, she'll need to miss it to rest. *Doctor's* orders."

A commotion at the front entrance causes us to step apart and turn. A man I recognize as the well-known shipping mogul Carl Preston bursts through the doors with an older woman, whom I assume is his wife, hot on his heels.

"Where is she? Where's my Rhiannon?"

"Mr. Preston." Judge Carmichael turns to the man. "She's in there." He jerks his head toward her room.

"What the *fuck* happened?"

I watch as the woman rushes into Rhiannon's room and embraces her. It's clear these people are her parents, and I'm shocked I didn't recognize their daughter sooner. I've seen pictures of the three of them in the newspaper many times, especially while I was in college, but never in person. And though the woman, Mrs. Preston, has gray hair and the years show on her face, she's the older version of the woman lying in the bed.

"She tripped and took a spill down the stairs, Mr. Preston. This is Dr. Gage Winston. He's one of the top orthopedic surgeons in the nation. Dr. Winston, please let me introduce Mr. Preston—Rhiannon's father."

"Mr. Preston. I've heard a lot about you in the paper." Gage shakes his hand. "This is my brother, Drake Winston. We were together when I got the call, so he came along for the ride. Your daughter is going to be just fine, even though she broke the radius in her left arm. It won't require surgery but will need to be immobilized. There is a possibility she'll need some physical therapy, but I won't know for certain for a couple of weeks."

"Thank God. I was scared out of my wits when my wife got the call from your groundskeeper."

I cut my eyes to Judge Carmichael. "*You* didn't call him?"

"I was more concerned with my wife," he spits out, his eyes filled with venom.

"And what do *you* do, Mr. Winston?" The question is addressed to me by her father, who stares at me with interest. "You obviously know I own Preston Shipping, yet I'm not sure I know anything about you."

"I own Angel's Wings—an organization for people who can't or don't have the ability to grasp second chances when they've been living in hell." My gaze travels to Judge Carmichael as I say the last part.

"Right." Her father holds my gaze for longer than I care before looking back to Gage. "You're Calvin Winston's boys, aren't you?"

"Unfortunately," Gage interrupts. "If you'll excuse us. Drake." Gage motions for me to follow him.

Gage shakes his head, the irritation prevalent on his face. "Those two are the most pretentious pricks I've ever met in my life."

Raising one eyebrow, I nudge him with a knowing look. "Where are you going?"

"My office. I need to take a minute to write up my notes. Maybe by the time I'm done, his wife's scans will be done." We board the elevator and travel up to the third floor where Gage's office is located.

"And you think she tripped down the stairs like they're claiming?"

"No." Gage growls. "Her break is certainly consistent with falling down a flight of stairs. But the massive lump on the back of her head doesn't match her version of what happened."

"What's *her* version?" I seat myself in the chair opposite Gage's desk as he closes the door.

"Both of them say she tripped going down the steps. Mrs. Carmichael says she put her arms out to brace her fall and went down them headfirst, breaking her arm as she landed on it. However, the lump on the back of her head says differently. Skulls don't just bruise without direct, blunt force trauma. And her break looks like she tried to grab the railing and twisted her arm as she fell. That, along with the cut to her temple with the bruises—bruises that look an awful lot like fingerprints, paired with the hematoma to her skull on the back that her husband has failed to mention, indicates she fell backward, not forward."

"*Fuck.*"

Gage nods as he drops into his own chair and slides his hands through his hair. "Yep. I'm pretty sure she was pushed. Or at a minimum, if she *did* fall, she was turned to block a blow to the face following several others that had already hit their mark."

My leg bounces with unease. This is the shit we try to help women escape. "Did you ask her?"

"In a roundabout way. Her husband's a fucking judge—not to mention a huge financial donor to the hospital. I have to tread lightly about this."

"You think he's hurting her." It's more a statement, as I don't need to voice it as a question, not when we've both seen it before.

Gage runs his palm down his face. "I do."

There's a slight tap at the door before it's pushed open. "Dr. Winston. That patient you asked us to notify you of—the one that came in a few days ago. She's back."

"I gotta go." Gage jolts up. "Call me later."

I stop him at the door, cocking my head at him. "Do you need me to come down with you?"

"No. But can you do me a favor?"

Gage is frazzled as he rushes down the hallway—something he's never done. Whatever is going on with this patient, it has him tangled up in ways I haven't witnessed before. It's nearing one a.m., which means Roland should be done. I tug my phone out and press his contact.

"Hey. Everything okay at the hospital?" His voice sounds tired.

"Define okay. The judge's wife fell down the stairs and broke her arm. You still feel like grabbing a drink?" I don't feel like talking about the shitty judge over the phone.

Roland sighs, "Can I get a raincheck? I'm beat and I have something I need to deal with."

Flicking at fuzz on my jacket, I nod to nobody in particular. "Yeah, okay. When are you back in Atlanta?"

"Two weeks. My last show is in Austin next weekend. Then I'm done for a bit."

I can hear someone's muffled voice in the background, then the sound of something brushing against the phone as I assume Roland covers it to say something to whoever is there with him. I can't make out his words, but I can tell the person he's talking to is crying.

"Roland, are you okay?"

He hesitates for a moment before answering, and it isn't convincing when he does. "Yeah, sorry. Look, I need to go. Tell Gage I'll catch up later."

"You'd tell me if you needed help, right?" I frown at the phone and the hinky feeling that swells in my gut.

"It's nothing, Drake, but I need to take care of this."

I groan, but sigh heavily into the receiver. "Yeah, okay. Call me this week. Be safe, Rol. Love you."

I fist my phone and stare at the screen. What the hell is happening with my siblings? Both seem to be dealing with something they're clearly holding close to the chest. I press the button for the elevator and wait for it to arrive, my head spinning the whole time with the night's events—more specifically on the woman still laid up in the ER.

The doors ding, signaling my arrival on the first floor. My thoughts are so preoccupied with Judge Carmichael and his wife that I don't notice him standing in the hallway.

"Mr. Winston." He blocks my path. "Please tell your brother thank you. He seems to be tied up at the moment or I'd tell him myself."

I move around him, making my way toward the exit. "Sure. Have a good night, Judge."

"I look forward to seeing you next weekend."

Right. The gala. I'd be lying if I said I was looking forward to the event—because I'm not. I hate being around the elitists that think they can buy their way out of everything. Even though my brothers and I have money, we never let it make us pompous assholes. Sure, we like nice things, but we don't use it to buy our way out of trouble—at least not at the expense of others.

My eyes catch sight of Gage. He's embracing a woman inside one of the patient rooms. She's crying her eyes out as he holds her, his hand stroking her head as he whispers some-thing into her ear. I can't hear what he's saying, but it's obvious she is in distress. His piercing cerulean orbs lock with mine and he doesn't blink as he holds my gaze. He doesn't need to speak. I get the message without words. The woman in his arms is in trouble… and from the looks of it, so is my brother.

I dip my chin at him and hurry outside, the nighttime breeze biting at my skin as I make my way to my car. There's a strange vibe bursting in the air. An ominous one that leaves me plagued with anxiety. I can't place my finger on what I'm feeling, but I know whatever it is—it's big. Both of my siblings seem to be hiding something that they aren't ready to share.

Thoughts of them lead me down a rabbit hole of confusion, making me immediately think of Judge Carmichael's wife, Rhiannon. My heart gallops beneath my ribs, creating a pressure beneath the flesh that makes it hard to breathe. I want to storm back inside and save her from the monster standing at the foot of her bed. And that scares the shit out of me. Deciding I need a distraction from my unease, I turn my car toward the one place I feel in control—the club.

The moment I step inside the space, the unmistakable thrum of desire scorches through my veins. This is just what I need to regain a sense of self. I head toward the bar and order a shot of whiskey, but no sooner does the bartender set the glass in front of me than a dainty hand presses against my forearm.

"Wasn't expecting to see you so soon." Kat slides in beside me at the bar.

Giving her the side eye, I down the amber liquid, letting it fill my gut with a warmth that makes me heat in more ways than one. "Let's go."

I make my way toward a private room, not bothering to see if she's following.

"Wait." She calls out from behind me, halting my forward motion. "Can another woman join us?"

I raise an eyebrow at her. I don't mind the thought of someone joining in, but I'm the one who decides. Hearing her ask almost pisses me off. I growl under my breath but push my frustration aside and nod. "Meet me in the room in five minutes. If you're late, I'll leave."

"Yes, sir." Her compliance makes my cock pulse with need.

The room is bathed in a red glow from a couple of lamps placed throughout the space. I'm grateful the room is unoccupied, as it has become my favorite. I pull the cotton shirt I'm wearing over my head and toss it to a nearby chair. After kicking off my shoes and removing my socks, tonight, I need to lose myself for just a little while.

A slight creak of the door makes me glance over my shoulder. Kat is followed by a woman that makes me pause. Even though she too has her face covered, the uncanny resemblance to the judge's wife is still obvious. Her long brown hair cascades over her bare shoulders, leading to a narrow frame. The black corset she wears does little to conceal the ample bosom beneath it. Like Kat's, I suspect her tits aren't real.

I move toward the two women, both standing perfectly still, waiting for my commands.

"Did Kat explain my rules?" I watch her quick intake of breath as my fingers trail down her bare arm.

"Yes, sir." Her timid response makes me smirk as I continue my appraisal of her body.

"Good. Don't move." I circle her, taking in every square inch of exposed skin. "Kat, I want you to kneel before her."

Kat silently moves in front of her and drops to her knees. She bows her head, waiting for my instructions. I finger the ribbons holding the black corset onto the woman's body and tug them loose. The material drops to the ground beside Kat with a thud, leaving her bare except for the black satin thong she wears. My palm cups her breast as my thumb swipes over her pert nipple. Leaning forward, I circle the pink bud with my tongue. "Pull her panties down." I bark out my first order and watch as Kat slips the smooth material down her thin legs and tosses them away from us. "Lick her pussy, Kat."

The moment Kat's tongue connects with her center, the stranger's body tenses. I don't ask her name, because I don't need to know it for what I am about to do to her. I pinch her nipple between my thumb and pointer finger, eliciting a sharp inhale of breath from her and a slight falter in her stance.

"Don't move." I swat at her ass, pissed she didn't hold still—even *if* it was only slight.

"Yes, sir." She dips her head in acknowledgement of fucking up.

Looking down at Kat, I watch as she attacks her core with fervor. I wrap my fingers in Kat's blonde strands and tug her head back. "Stop. She will not come."

My palm trails down the woman's body and stops at her slit. Her pussy is dripping wet with a mixture of Kat's spit and her own juices. My finger glides between her folds with ease as I push it inside her channel. Her body starts to quiver from the forceful intrusion. As I pump in and out, I pull harder on

Kat's hair. I'm demanding as I push her head toward my groin. "Take my cock out and suck me off."

Kat's delicate hand seeks out my zipper, dragging it down to release my manhood. I stiffen beneath her touch as she tugs me out from the confines of my pants and covers my hard member with her mouth.

"Fuck." I hiss, bucking my hips into her face. The woman I'm fingering lets out a moan and I jerk my hand free, withholding the orgasm I know she's close to. I close my eyes and focus on Kat's lips wrapped around my shaft. Jamming my hand back between the stranger's legs, I twist my hand, reaching for the rough spot inside her. "I know you want to scream. But I don't allow it." It's mean but getting her close to cut her off is what control is all about.

"Stop." I move out of Kat's grasp and pull my fingers from the nameless girl's hole. Licking her essence from my fingers, I move toward the bed, kicking my pants off as I do. "Get on the bed. Both of you."

Kat and her friend scramble toward the massive king size bed and crawl on.

"Kat, take your clothes off."

She disrobes quickly and lays back, baring herself to me. Both women lie side by side, awaiting my next order. I tug at my new pet's legs, pulling her until she's positioned at the edge of the mattress. I jam my finger between her folds with such force her entire body shakes.

"Kat." I motion for her to crawl toward me and straddle the girl's head. "Ride here face." I flick Kat's clit, pinching and rolling it between my fingers before stepping back. After retrieving a few things, I reposition myself between her thighs.

I cover my cock in a rubber and thrust inside her cunt. Kat is moaning above her, lost in the rapture of the girl's tongue in her center. I lean forward, placing my mouth at the juncture of Kat's legs. The heat of the stranger's pussy wrapped around my cock, combined with the taste of Kat on my lips, is maddening.

I use the vibrator I set to the side, pressing it to the spot where my body is joined with hers. It's like a match being thrown into a vat of gasoline, igniting a firestorm beneath me. Her body arches as her legs tighten around me. My cock swells inside her hole, threatening to rip through the condom if I don't slow my driving thrusts. Just as she starts to lose all control, I jerk the vibrator from her clit. Her body tenses, but her release never comes.

I can see the confusion in her eyes, but I ignore it, pounding into her as I chase my release. My balls tighten and I let go, spilling myself inside the tiny barrier buried in her cunt. My mouth parts and I cry out my release, uttering one simple word. One that burns into my conscious leaving me feeling more fucked up than ever.

"Rhiannon."

I withdraw my cock and step away from the pair, who are panting heavily on the bed. "Get dressed and get out." I bark my order as I flee to the bathroom. I don't give a fuck that I only took what I needed from them.

I turn on the shower and step in once the water is heated. With my palms braced against the tiled wall, I hang my head. I needed the release to push down the foreign emotions I've been feeling since meeting the woman whose name I just cried out. Being the cold-hearted bastard in there makes me feel more like myself. So, I'd like to believe. But as the water flows over my body and swirls its escape down the drain, only one thing—or rather, one person fills my thoughts.

Rhiannon.

6

Drake

THE ALARM CLOCK from my phone tears me from my fitful night's rest. I've been plagued with dreams of a woman who is off limits. Pushing myself up, I sit on the edge of the bed and rub my face. My cock is hard and tenting the sheet that's covering my hips. Even in sleep, my dick hasn't gotten the memo that Rhiannon is forbidden. It's disconcerting how much she affects me from a single meeting. A meeting that was awkward and brief.

I toss the sheet aside and stride to my bathroom. A cold shower sounds like the best medicine to rid myself of my current predicament. I turn the water on and step in before giving it time to heat.

The first needles of spray cause me to wince in shock. "Fuck." I mutter into the stall as I brace my hand against the cool tile and force myself to endure the icy deterrent. With my head bowed beneath the stream of water, I close my eyes and drift back to the dream that had me tossing and turning in the dark.

"Do you love me?" I brush a stray strand of hair from her face.

"I don't know." She turns her gaze to the floor. "Would it be wrong if I did? I'm still a married woman."

I grip her chin with my fingers and drag her eyes up to meet mine. "The only thing wrong would be denying what you know. I'll ask you again, Rhi. Do. You. Love. Me?"

Her eyes fill with tears and a single tear slips from her lashes. I swipe the bead with my thumb and press my lips to hers. I don't need her to say it—I already know.

"Drake." She whimpers against my lips. "I'm scared."

"Scared of what?" I kissed down her jaw, nibbling at her soft flesh below her ear.

"That I'll wake up and still be trapped."

My eyes snap open at the memory or hidden omen. I couldn't possibly allow myself to get tangled up with her—even if my cock wept at the mere thought of the stranger. After soaping myself up, I rinse the suds and cut off the water. My cock has finally noticed I'm not going to give in and begun softening.

My hand brushes the fog from the mirror, and I stare at my reflection. I wouldn't let myself have romantic love, instead I devoted myself to freeing others from relationships that resembled the one I'd grown-up watching from the sidelines. That's why I devote myself to the work I do. I couldn't save my mother, but I will save any woman who comes to me for help. It's the only way I can atone for the loss of my mom.

Just as I'm finishing my morning routine, my cell rings. I'm surprised to see Archer, head of my security company, calling me on a Sunday.

"Archer." I hit the speaker button and continue trimming my beard.

"Drake, sorry to bother you on a Sunday. But I have that information you requested. The one your brother asked about."

"Right. She was admitted to the hospital last night." I wipe my face off and carry the phone into my bedroom. "I should call Gage and see what happened."

"No need. I talked with him earlier this morning. Her name is Poppy, twenty-four, and are you ready for this?" Archer's tone grows serious. "She's Alessandro Hugo's sister."

"Fuck." Gage couldn't have picked a worse person to help. Alessandro Hugo is known for being involved in illegal business dealings. "Does Gage know?"

"Yes. Apparently, she's in a relationship with Hugo's head of security. Poppy has her mother's last name, which is how she's flown under the radar when making her trips to the ER. No one associated her with Hugo."

"Gage can't get involved with this one. Alessandro is not a man to fuck around with—neither is his henchman, Eduardo. I need to call him."

"I think it's a little late for that." Archer blows out a breath.

"What do you mean?"

"Drake, Gage called me this morning to secure a safe house for her. He took her there about an hour ago."

"Please tell me you're joking. Gage took a woman he barely knows, one that's tied to a deranged man who would slit his throat over brunch, to a safe house?"

"'Fraid so." Archer grows quiet. "There's more. He's with her."

My blood heats with irritation as I ask incredulously, "What do you mean he's *with* her?"

"Gage patched her up in the ER—and then discharged her this morning. Only she didn't get in the car with her security. She got in Gage's car."

I groan as the blood drains from my face. "God damn it. What is he *doing*?"

"I don't know. This isn't like your brother. He doesn't get invested in anyone long term."

"The fucking Gala is this weekend. People are going to notice him missing and that spells trouble."

"You'll figure it out. Call him, though. She needs to get out of that relationship or it's going to kill her. That woman has been in the hospital or urgent care twenty times in the last year. I get why he did it, just don't approve of his methods."

"Shit." I rub my hand down my face. "Thanks Archer. Keep me posted."

My phone bounces off the bed and hits the floor when I toss it. Gage is the level head of the three of us. This is so far out of character for him, I'm not sure what to make of it. I dress in a pair of jeans, a t-shirt, and tennis shoes, needing to feel some form of relaxation. Sunday is the day I usually visit with Julie, our aunt. Outside of my brothers, she's the only person I care about.

I retrieve my cell phone from the floor, relieved to see I haven't damaged it in my fit of rage. I need to call Gage, but first, I need coffee. My apartment overlooks the city skyline. I had it built to my exact desires. Not that anyone ever comes up here aside from my brothers. If I need sex, I go to the club. Bringing a woman here implies something more than physical, so I steer clear of doing that. My office is below my living quarters, allowing me quick access if someone needs to meet with me.

As the first sip of black gold passes my lips, I shudder. There are three things in life I drink—Whiskey, water and black coffee. Nothing else passes my lips or enters my temple. I pride myself on taking care of my body. When I can't go to the club to relieve tension, I'm at the gym. Nothing gets my blood pumping like a good run or hitting the weights... well, except a tight pussy around my shaft. *Fuck.* Thoughts of sex have steered my brain back to Rhiannon.

Needing a distraction, I push aside my own dilemma and dial my brother. He has some explaining to do and it better be good. Gage has gotten himself tangled up with the worst possible woman on the planet. It rings twice before he picks up.

"Gage, what in the fuck are you doing?" I snap.

"I know you're pissed—"

I cut him off. "*Pissed?*" I huff out a laugh, the sound manic. "Pissed doesn't even cover it. Do you realize who that woman is? Why *her*, Gage? You've helped hundreds of women over the years. What makes this one different?"

"I can't explain it, Drake. But I need to make sure she's safe. I've taken a leave of absence from the hospital. I need you to cover for me at the Gala."

"Do you hear yourself? *Fuck.*" I pinch the bridge of my nose and take some calming breaths. "Her brother is a sick motherfucker, Gage. If he doesn't come for you, her boyfriend will. Are you ready to deal with that? Do you have a *death wish?*"

"I need you to file the appropriate paperwork to protect her. She needs out of that life and out from under her brother's thumb. He doesn't care about her wellbeing or the fact his right-hand man is beating her. And I'm going to help her— whatever that means. One day you'll understand."

"Understand what?"

"Poppy has been coming into my ER for months, Drake. I couldn't stand by and watch him kill her. She's too scared to go to the police. This was the only way."

"Then bring her here. Let me set her up with Angel's Wings. My people can help her start over."

"No. I'm helping her. Look." I could hear Gage shuffling in the background. "She's waking up. I need to make sure she's good. I'll call you later. And Drake?" His voice drops to a whisper. "Please do this for me."

"Fine. I'll call you when I have everything done. Be careful, brother. I feel you're getting in deeper than you realize, and it'll be too late to undo it." I sigh into the phone, knowing I will not win the argument with him.

"It's already too late. I'll talk to you soon."

The phone cut off, leaving me to stare at the blackened screen. This wasn't the brooding older brother I know. Something is different. I dump my cup into the sink and grab my keys. I need to draw up the paperwork for Poppy's divorce, and I'd rather do that from the comfort of my office. Plus, I'll have access to my desktop which holds all the templates for the divorce order.

I take the elevator down and smile when I step onto the office floor and find Alex Whitmire in his office. He's my age and just as much a work addict as me. The only difference is he has a girlfriend. I don't know why she's stuck around for this long, seeing as he is always here and not with her.

"Working? On a Sunday?" I lean against the doorframe to his office, laughing when his head snaps up from his computer screen.

"Yeah. I have that big court case tomorrow and need to finish a few things." He leans back in his seat and stretches. "What about you? You don't normally come in on Sunday."

"My brother Gage is helping a woman get out of a bad situation. I'm drawing up her paperwork today."

"Wow. She must be important if you're doing that now. Couldn't it have waited until Monday?" He tilts his head in question.

"She's Alessandro Hugo's sister'." His entire frame shifts from being relaxed to on alert.

"You aren't serious."

"Unfortunately, I wish I wasn't. But it would appear my brother has gotten himself involved in a mess."

"Well, if you need my help with anything, just ask. Anything involving Alessandro Hugo isn't going to be a run-of-the-mill case. To him, women are property and I imagine his sister is no different." Alex taps his hand on the desk. "Hopefully, Gage won't need my services." He smirks.

"Let's pray not." I smile and turn. "Don't stay too long. I imagine your girlfriend would like to see you at some point."

"Actually, we broke up." He fakes a smile, but I can tell he is hurting from the words.

"Sorry to hear that." I pause.

"Work is more important—at least according to her." He sighs. "She's probably right. Anyway. Let me know if you need something."

I leave his office and stare at my computer screen. Archer emailed all the information he dug up on Poppy, making it easy to do the needed documents. Since I assumed her main goal was to get out, I draft up the protection order, asking for standard guidelines. My organization will help her find somewhere to live and possibly get a job. I notice she'd been in college when she found herself tangled up with her brother's henchman, causing her to drop out. Perhaps she'd want to go back once she's free of him. Alex was right—Hugo treats people like his property. He likely made her quit to maintain control over her. And his idea of control was letting his head of security beat the shit out of her whenever the mood struck him.

If there's ever been a woman who needed a safe exit, it's her. This isn't going to be easy though—just serving the papers to Alessandro is going to trigger a chain of events that I'm not sure Gage is entirely ready for. Nor will anyone be able to stop them once it's begun. We need to make sure he's hidden and well protected as well. I can't risk losing him to another monster's hands.

Archer is the only person I trust to ensure their safety if— let's be serious, *when*—this shit goes sideways. I press the stored number on my desk phone and wait.

"Drake. Two calls on a Sunday must mean something big." Archer's voice is smooth as silk and almost taunting. It's like he knows me too well.

Setting aside the gnawing sensation in my gut, I lay it on the line. "Archer, I need to know my brother is secure. I plan on filing the papers tomorrow, which means Alessandro Hugo will be notified in a few days. He's going to lose his shit and stop at nothing to find his sister. I'm surprised he hasn't already beaten down the hospital doors searching for her."

There's a couple clicks that no doubt come from Archer's mouth like he's about to scold a small child, "Actually, that's already happened. Her security guard suspected something was off when she didn't come back from x-ray. My contacts tell me his people are searching for her now. The only good news is they haven't attached Gage to her disappearance —yet."

"That's not going to last. I want your best guys on Gage. We need to be prepared for anything."

"Don't worry. I have him stashed somewhere they won't find him."

I twirl the cord in my hand and wait." Where is he?"

"How about you worry about the paperwork, and I'll worry about your brother? The less you know, the better. Can't get blood out of a turnip, am I right? If you don't know, the less likely someone can put pressure on you to give him up."

I don't like it. Not knowing where my eldest brother is, gives me a hollow feeling in my chest. "I don't know, Archer. I trust you implicitly, but not knowing—"

"All you need to know is he is not in this state. I have him tucked away with some friends who, like me, protect individuals. Honestly." Archer pauses. "They might be even better than me."

I grunt with acknowledgement that he's right. "Fine. I want to know the minute something changes, or any contact attempts are made."

"You got it. Let me know when you file the papers, so I can be on standby. Crazy people tend to get crazier when they feel threatened, and I need to know when to make popcorn."

I disconnect the phone and sigh. It won't take much for Hugo or his asshole associate to figure out Gage is involved. He's the attending orthopedic doctor in the ER and was there when she came in. Hell, her security most likely saw his face. There's no way to hide that he played a role somehow.

I wanted to strangle my brother. What the *fuck* was he thinking?

7

Drake

JUST AS I EXPECTED, Gage's mess is turning into a nightmare of epic proportions. Court services failed to notify me when papers were served, which led to the man currently standing in the lobby of my building, raising hell. Max, my head of security, is about two seconds from tossing him out on his ass. Which means *I* need to get down there pronto before things turn into something akin to the final scene at Pelennor Fields, minus the well-trained armies.

The elevator opens and my vision fills with the man himself. *Alessandro Hugo.* He's being held in place by Max, his arms flailing around like a raging bull trying to break free from his pen.

"Mr. Hugo." I nod toward the front desk receptionist, letting her know we have the situation under control for now. "Is there something you need?" While I know without a doubt he's here because his lackey has probably been served with the restraining order, I play like I'm clueless.

"Don't play dumb with me, you prick." His spittle goes everywhere as he speaks. "Where's my fucking sister?"

Leaning against the wall, I bring one hand up to my face as I pretend to check my fingernails for dirt. "I assume your friend received my paperwork?"

"Yeah, he got your fucking papers." He jerks out of Max's hold and straightens his suit coat. "Where is she? I want to talk to my sister about these so-called accusations she's making."

"So-called?" I cock an eyebrow at him. "There is nothing so-called about her petition for a protection order. And as far as where she is…" I choose my next words carefully. " I honestly can't tell you."

"The fuck you can't," he spits as he lunges at me, getting around my security's massive frame somehow. I spin out of his trajectory and wrap my arm around his neck. With his momentum, I drop him to his knees and squeeze my arm around his throat.

Clearing my throat, I sigh like I'm bored. "Now you can calm down, or I'll call the cops and let them deal with you. I don't think you want that, seeing as the reason for the petition is based on years of physical abuse."

Alessandro Hugo stops moving beneath my hold and grunts. "Let me go, hijo de puta."

"I'll show you how much of a mother fucker I can be, Mr. Hugo—in court. Now," I loosen my hold on him and step back. "Get the fuck out of my building. You're not welcome here again."

I watch as Max drags Hugo from the lobby and tosses him onto the street outside. This is the problem I'm afraid of—dealing with Hugo and his lackeys. Gage truly stepped in it this time—and for what, I still don't understand. Us Winston men don't get involved with women. This shit is a prime example of why.

"Do *not* let that man in the building again. For any reason. Use force if necessary to prevent his entry, Max."

I spin on my heel and beeline toward the elevator. Gage isn't the only thing I need to worry about today — I'm due in court in less than an hour. Thankfully, the case I'm finally closing out today is an easy one. The husband of my client didn't contest the divorce and has essentially agreed to everything but alimony, which is why we're heading to court. Now and then, I get a couple who just don't love each other anymore—and this is one of them.

After retrieving my briefcase and all the needed documents, I toss the satchel over my shoulder and make my way back down to the lobby. Glancing at my watch, I grin when I realize I still have forty minutes before I need to report to the courtroom, which gives me enough time to get *fully* caffeinated.

I hop into my Challenger and pull out onto the street, pointing it in the courthouse's direction. After parking it in one of the nearby garages, I grab my bag and make my way toward the little bistro down from court services.

The moment I step inside, I'm assaulted by the thick aroma of coffee beans and pastries, but that's not what stops me dead in my tracks. No—it's the vision sitting in the back corner alone. I blink, trying to clear the shock of seeing Rhiannon Carmichael seated by herself. Making my way to the counter, I can't help but look over my shoulder to ensure she's actually there as I wait for my drink. The cashier takes my money, offering to bring it to me at my table when he sees who I'm staring at.

"I'll be over there, at the table with the woman in the corner." He gives me a knowing grin and nods as I turn and walk toward her. Her head snaps up as I near the table and I see a flash of fear in her eyes as she scans the crowded shop.

"Hello, Mrs. Carmichael. I don't know if you recall seeing me —my brother is Gage Winston, erm, Dr. Winston. I was with him the night you were in the ER. How are you?"

Her skin flushes at the mention of my brother - most likely from embarrassment. "Oh. No, I don't remember you." She takes a deep breath and forces a smile. "I was probably doped up that night." She holds up the arm, now covered in a bright pink cast.

"Right. You fell down the steps and broke it, right? Sorry, I'm Drake, by the way." I motion to the empty seat. "May I join you?"

She swallows, her eyes scanning the shop again before nodding. I have this overwhelming need to reach across the table and take her free hand in mine to comfort her. I can tell my sitting here is making her nervous, and I need to know why.

"Is me sitting here a problem?" I glance around, trying to see who she's looking for.

She twists her hair between her fingers. "Um. I don't think so. You know my husband, right?"

"Yes. I do." The cashier drops my coffee and pastry on the table in front of me. I grip the hot paper cup in my hand and press it to my mouth, blowing on it slightly before taking a sip. "In fact, I am due in his courtroom in about, oh—" I glance at my watch "—twenty minutes."

"You're an attorney." She holds my gaze as she states the obvious.

"Yes. Divorce." I bite the pastry, the filling oozing out onto my lip. Rhiannon watches as I lick the jelly substance off my face and then blot the spot with my napkin. "What about you? What do you do?"

She swallows, her eyes still on the spot I just touched with my tongue as she speaks. "Nothing. I do nothing. Not anymore, at least. Heath doesn't like the idea of me working outside the house—so when we got married, I had to give up my dream of teaching."

"You gave it up for him?"

She nods slightly. "I didn't have a choice." The way her voice dips causes my breath to hitch in my lungs.

"You seem a lot younger than Heath." I watch her shift nervously in her seat at my intrusive statement.

She nods again, her blonde head almost like a cheap souvenir bobblehead that's slightly broken. "I'm thirty and Heath is fifty-five."

I mull over her admission, searching for the right thing to say. A twenty-five-year difference is shocking—especially for a woman like her. A woman who can have any man she wants. She can see the shock on my face, and sighs.

She frowns like she's expecting me to judge her, "I know you're probably wondering why I would marry such an older man—but it was something my parents set up."

"Like an arranged marriage? You realize it's the twenty-first century, right? Arranged marriages aren't exactly something we do in this day and age." I grunt, irritated that this woman would subject herself to something so barbaric.

Her face morphs into an expression of anger, and she pushes back her chair and stands. "I've spent the last year listening to a man tell me I'm worthless, so listening to one I barely know regurgitate similar garbage is not something I care to do. Have a good day, Mr. Winston."

Rhiannon turns to leave, but I reach up and grab her hand. The minute our palms touch, an electric pulse courses through my veins. I know she feels it too, because the quick intake of breath and the dilation of her pupils give her reaction away.

"Wait." I finger out my business card and press it between our joined hands. "If you ever need anything, here's my number."

She holds my gaze for what feels like an eternity before crumbling the card and jamming it into her pocket and turning away. She storms through the tiny café and hurries outside onto the curb. It's impossible to pull my eyes away, even though I know I should. My gut churns with this burning desire to chase after her, but I remain frozen to the spot.

The sound of my cell cuts through the fog surrounding me, crashing my thoughts to a sudden halt.

"*What?*" I snap into the phone.

"Damn, brother." Roland's voice comes through the line, making my tension evaporate into thin air. "What's got you so pissy?"

"Headed to court. You know how I get." I play it off, not wanting to talk about my fucked-up feelings right this minute. "To what do I owe the pleasure of this unexpected call?"

Roland's voice is playful, but there's something hidden in his tone. "Har har… I just wanted to update you on my arrival. I know I told you I was coming home in a few weeks, but something has come up and I won't make it right away."

My hackles go up immediately. "Is everything ok?"

He clears his throat and plays it off like it's nothing. "Yes. Of course. I just need to take care of some things regarding my publicist—then I'll be home for a while."

His blasé tone does nothing to assuage the bad feeling. "A while?"

"Yeah. I'm burned out and need a long break. But don't worry, I'm fine. I tried to call Gage, but he didn't answer. Can you let him know about the change in plans?"

Sighing, I nod, even though he can't see me. "Yeah, Gage is tied up right now, but I'll pass on the info. Call me if you need something, Roland."

"Will do—love you, bro."

Shoving the device in my pocket, I hurry from the café toward the courthouse. I need to get this case completed so I can focus on the shitshow my brother has now stirred up from the bowels of hell. As soon as I enter the building, I find my client—Lori Conrad. She's waiting on me along with her soon to be ex-husband beside her.

"You ready to get this over with?" I direct my question to her, ignoring him.

She nods with an exasperated sigh. "Yes. Do we really have to go into the courtroom?"

I cut my eyes to him. "Have you agreed to the alimony?"

He blows out a breath and nods. "Yes. I just want this to be over so we can move on with our lives."

My eyebrow arches and suspicion worms its way into my thoughts. "Why so suddenly?"

His face pales, and I can see the hesitation in his eyes. "I… huh. I guess I'm ready to start over and having this held over my head keeps either of us from doing that."

I glance at my client, whose expression reeks of irritation and disgust. "Can we speak privately?" She closes her eyes and blows out a breath, giving me a slight nod. "We'll be back in a moment."

She follows me to a small conference room near the courtroom and steps inside. "Why the sudden change?"

Hanging her head, her voice suddenly grows meek. "I'm tired, Mr. Winston. He won't stop calling and begging me to agree, so he can move on. I think—" she swallows loudly. "I think he's met someone."

I nod as I clear my throat. "I see. And you're willing to just forgo everything you deserve and let him have his cake?"

"Yes… no. Fuck, I don't know what to do." She shakes her head. "I asked for this divorce because he wasn't making any effort in the marriage. I know my job as a nurse is demanding, but I just thought we were growing apart—but maybe…"

I sigh, trying to deliver my words gently, though the words don't seem to come as a surprise to her. "Maybe it's been another woman the entire time. You said it was amicable and didn't need any digging done, so I didn't. But if he's been having an affair, that changes things."

"I don't think I have it in me to care. I just want this over."

I shake my head as I grab her shoulders gently. "I understand, but we aren't signing those papers the way he wants them. Do you trust me?"

Her head pops up from where she had been looking at her feet, and I see the unspilled tears in her eyes. "Yes."

"Then don't say a word and go along with what I say and do. Understand?"

"Ok."

We step out of the room and find her husband waiting by the courtroom we are scheduled to enter in less than fifteen minutes.

With a righteous smirk on my face, I announce triumphantly, "Alright, Mr. Conrad. This is how it's going to go. We'll sign papers to avoid the courtroom, but you're going to sign the original decree."

Her husband's face blanches as he shakes his head, "No. I won't agree to give her that much. This was supposed to be amicable. How is it amicable if she's getting alimony?"

"The alimony is going to pay for the years of giving herself to a man who clearly didn't love her. And if you refuse, we will walk into court, and I'll call your girlfriend to the stand."

A look of horror passes over his face when I utter the words. While I don't actually know if he's been having an affair the entire time, he doesn't know that. And based on his reaction, I assume I've hit a nerve.

"Uh." He glances at his soon-to-be ex-wife and sighs. "Fine. I'll sign. Can we just keep her out of this?"

"You've got to be fucking kidding me." Lora grunts. "How long, Bill?"

He palms the back of his neck. "Three years."

Her voice rises an octave. "Wow. We've been married *ten*. Not to mention we only stopped having sex a year ago."

I pull the papers out of my briefcase and hand them over to him. "Where's your attorney?"

"Inside waiting."

I smirk and motion to the courtroom. "Go get him and let him know you're signing. I will let the clerk know we've reached an agreement."

I watch as he heads into the courtroom before turning to my client. "I know this sucks... but you'll be able to start over— and maybe find someone who deserves you. Don't settle this time. Find a man who makes you—his whole world."

I glare at the man, who returns with the signed documents and snatch them out of his hands. I start toward the clerk's office to turn over the decree and pause when Lora gets my attention.

"Thank you, Mr. Winston, for everything." She closes her eyes and breathes out. "Whatever woman manages to get a ring from you is going to be one lucky girl."

"That will be impossible..." I pause briefly. "Because I am never getting married."

8

Drake

I FUCKING HATE THESE THINGS—WHEN I get my hands on Gage… I'm going to kill him. He owes me big because he's the one typically schmoozing these pretentious assholes. And right now, I'm having to listen to some suit who thinks he's better than us—the Winston brothers. He knew my father, which means he only knows the shitty side of the family and assumes we're just like him.

"Where is the glorified Dr. Winston, anyway?"

My head snaps up at the snarky question coming from the head of cardio, who is staring at me with an eyebrow cocked. "I'm sorry? Did you have something you needed, Charles?"

His voice is an attempt at superiority but comes across as bitterness. "I'm just surprised to see your brother taking a leave of absence from work. I assumed he didn't take time off for *pleasure*."

"Who said he was? Besides, what my brother does or doesn't do outside the walls of the hospital is not your concern. And as far as pleasure," I take a sip of the golden liquid sitting in front of me. "...I assure you the Winston boys get plenty."

Charles Peters grunts, swirling the clear drink he's been nursing all night. "Will he be making his typical donation?"

"Yes. In fact—" I push back in my chair to stand. "He's doubling it, as are Roland and me. Now, if you'll excuse me, I need to take care of something."

I leave him there choking on his tongue, and sure—Gage hadn't agreed to the increase in donation, but he'll get over it. The three of us have made good investments, turning the blood money our father left us into almost triple, leaving us billionaires at our young ages.

I push through the people gathering at the edge of the bar and make my way down the narrow hall toward the bathroom. I'm caught off guard when I round the corner to find Judge Carmichael leaning against the wall.

"Judge." I want to roll my eyes in disgust, but refrain. He's propped against the wall, staring at the ladies' room door. "Everything okay?"

"Yes. Waiting on Rhiannon to return. She had to 'powder her nose." He tips his head toward the closed door as he makes air quotations in the air with his fingers, but the irritation in his voice is palpable. "You know women."

"How's her arm doing?" I ask, even though I just saw her days before at that coffee shop and am well aware of her condition.

He shrugs his shoulders like he doesn't care. "Fine, I suppose. The cast is a hideous sight and I wish like hell she'd picked a different color."

I have to bite back the grin when I recall the fluorescent pink cast. I imagine it was her way of getting back at her uptight husband. As if on cue, Rhiannon emerges from the bathroom. It takes every ounce of my willpower to remain in place when I see the bruises from her supposed fall down the stairs marring her skin. When I ran into her at the cafe, her clothes had done a good job hiding the marks—but the gown she's wearing leaves a lot of skin exposed. Gage was right when he said they looked like fingerprints, because now, even days later, a light shade of blue and yellow make it obvious. And worse, she tried to cover them with makeup, but failed miserably.

"Mrs. Carmichael." I nod my head in greeting. "It's nice to see you again. How are you feeling?"

She pauses mid-step, her eyes flicking to her husband, who pins her in place with a venomous glare. "I'm fine. Thank you for asking."

I watch in complete horror as Judge Carmichael latches his slimy hand around her good arm and jerks her against him. Her face twists into a grimace, and I can see her fighting back tears. "Shut up, Rhiannon. You're embarrassing me right now."

I step forward, halting mere inches from him. "I'd suggest you take your hand off her like that, sir."

"Excuse me?" His head jerks toward me. "You mind your own damn business. She's *my* wife, and this is between us."

My heart skips a beat as a thunderous rage begins brewing inside my chest. "That may be true, but the way you just grabbed her isn't something I stand for - or any real man, for that matter. You're supposed to love and respect the woman you marry, not treat them like a possession. And *how* is she embarrassing you? I simply asked how she was doing, to which she answered."

He grumbles something unintelligible against her ear, making her body go rigid beside him. "I'm fine, Mr. Winston," she whispers softly, never breaking eye contact with me. "I need to go back to the lady's room. I left my purse." She pulls free and quickly disappears inside.

"You're just like my father. You think women are meant to be controlled, no matter the means." I brush past him, and shove open the men's room door. If I stand out there any longer, I'll undoubtedly put my hands on him—which wouldn't solve any problems.

After taking care of business and calming my raging nerves, I step into the hallway and plow over Rhiannon. "Shit." I grip her arms, steadying her in place. "Are you alright? I didn't see you."

She freezes beneath my touch, making me realize for the first time, my hands are on her body. I half-expect her to be shaking. Instead, heat radiates between us. Her eyes trace the point of contact, before meeting my shocked expression. "I..." she stutters, her eyes flicking between mine and where my hands rest against her. "I'm fine."

"Rhiannon," I mutter her name as my heart thunders inside my chest and the only sound I hear is the blood whooshing in my ears. "Is he hurting you?"

She laughs sourly as she shakes her head. "You're the one who nearly bowled me over."

Narrowing my gaze at her, I lower my voice as I clarify, "You know what I mean."

I see a flash of something in her eyes before she blinks it away. "It doesn't matter. You know who he is and what he's capable of."

It's not a denial, but she doesn't answer me. "It matters. You deserve better, Rhiannon."

"How can you say that? You don't know me or what I deserve." She jerks free, putting space between us. "I should go."

"Wait." I reach out and grab her arm again. "I don't know you —yet. You're right. But I know a woman like you deserves the world. And based on that pink cast and the bruises on your arms, I'd say you aren't getting that."

She sucks in a breath and glances back at me. "I gave up hopes of having the world the day I said, 'I do' to a monster."

"Let me help you," I plead, and step toward her.

"You can't. No one can." She wipes at a tear rolling down her cheek. "It was nice meeting you again, Mr. Winston."

I scan her face for signs of hope. "Hold on a second. Do you still have my card?"

"No. I threw it away so Heath wouldn't find it and beat me again."

I shove my hand in my pocket and yank out a business card. I always keep them on me for instances like this. I flip the card over and scribble my personal cell phone on the back. "Take this. If you change your mind or need help, call me. I'm serious, Rhiannon. I can protect you."

She reluctantly takes the card and stares at it for a moment. "Why are you doing this? He could ruin you." Rhiannon looks me in the eye and waits.

I clear my throat and answer honestly, "Because he's already trying to ruin you. There's something about you that draws me in. It's like you're the sun, and I'm desperately trying to touch it without getting burned." I reach out and brush a stray hair from her cheek. "You deserve a man who will worship you, not lock you away in a glass box. And I'm not afraid of your husband—that much I can promise you. I grew up with a man like him… and he didn't win, either."

Rhiannon blinks before nodding her head at me. "Good night, Mr. Winston." She folds the card in half and shoves it into the crevice of her cast as she walks away.

I wait to walk out, not wanting to give her husband any reason to unleash his wrath on her. When I emerge from the corridor, my eyes scan the room, seeking her out from the other guests. They land on her seated next to the judge, who stares in my direction. We glare at each other for a moment before I toss my hand up and wave. I need to leave before I do something epically dumb, like my brother—who *should* be here keeping me in check.

On cue, my phone vibrates in my pocket. Slipping it free, I see Archer's face flash across the screen.

"Archer." I bark into the line as I push my way through the throes of pretentious bodies lining the massive hall. Flashing one last glance in Rhiannon's direction, I smile when I catch her watching me in return.

"Drake, we have a new problem." Archer's irritated sigh says it's perhaps not news I'm going to like.

"What now?" I groan as I make my way toward my car.

"It seems Hugo has reached out to Roland."

"Fuck." Rage rises in my chest at the thought of Roland being dragged into this mess. "What did he tell him?"

"Drake." Archer sighs into the phone. "You need to meet me at the office. We don't need to discuss this over the phone."

"Fine. I'll be there in ten minutes." I toss the phone into the passenger seat as I slide behind the wheel. "*Fuck. Fuck Fuck fuckity fuck fuck.*"

I speed from the lot and practically break all the laws getting back to my building and parking haphazardly in my parking space. As soon as I enter, Archer is waiting for me in the lobby and the sight of him makes my stomach drop to my knees.

"What the fuck, Archer? Speak."

There's no sign of humor on Archer's face as he stares at me to deliver the news. "Hugo has taken an interest in Roland in hopes he would tell him where Gage was. Obviously, you haven't shared this with Roland, but he has now been dragged into this mess with Hugo, threatening him for information he obviously doesn't have. Have you talked to Roland lately?"

"No." I scrub my hand down my face. "Why? What did Roland say?"

Archer shakes his head. "Just that he had his own issues right now, and that he wasn't worried about Hugo."

Groaning, I slap a hand to my face and drag it down slowly. "Lovely. He has issues that are bad enough that he isn't worried about *Alessandro Hugo* being all up in his business. This is fucked up, Archer. Why the hell does it seem like my brothers are falling apart right now? And why in the hell is my *level-headed* brother risking his life for a stranger?"

"Love," Archer mumbles the word. "It does strange things to a man."

"Did you say 'love'?" I laugh at the idea that Gage is in love. "He barely knows her, not to mention we've sworn off that emotion. You know where it got my mother."

Frowning, Archer levels his gaze at me. "You're not your father, Drake. None of you are. And one day, a woman is going to prove that to you and you're going to stop at nothing to make her yours."

My thoughts immediately go to Rhiannon, and I pause. "So, what happens now?" I refuse to acknowledge his statement and change the subject to avoid the path he's steering this conversation down.

"You need to get this thing to court, like yesterday."

I rub my forehead in vexation and grunt. "It's on the docket for next month. It was the earliest I could make it happen."

Archer shakes his head, his forehead pinching in aggravation. "Make it sooner. Whoever you need to bribe, Drake. The longer we wait to bring this to a close, the more risk Gage faces."

"Fine, I'll make some calls in the morning. Everyone who matters is at the Gala—" I glance at my watch noting it's well after eleven pm. "—or in bed."

"Call me when you know something." Archer turns and stalks toward the entrance. He pauses briefly to glance over his shoulder. "I'll keep you updated."

Pressing the button to call the elevator down, I release a pessimistic breath as I step inside the metal box. This is a cluster fuck of epic proportions, and I don't know how I'm

going to make it disappear. I enter my apartment and immediately head for the kitchen. Grabbing a glass and my
whiskey, I pour a hefty sip. I strip off my tie as I go over the
events from tonight, my rage boiling close to the surface,
thinking about it all. I'm spent from my night pretending to
care about a bunch of assholes—the biggest being Judge
Carmichael.

After finishing the drink, I head to my room and strip off the
tux, exchanging it for a pair of gray sweats that hang loosely
against my hips. I've just crawled into bed when my phone
buzzes across the nightstand where I set it down. Picking it
up, I squint at the illuminated screen, seeing Max's icon, my
head of security here in the building.

Glancing at the time, I bite back the urge to cuss him out for
calling this late and hit the speaker button. "Max, it's after
midnight. What could be the problem now?"

"Sir." His voice filters through the speaker. "I know normally I
should call the hotline, but there's a woman here asking for
you."

I take him off speaker and press the phone to my ear as I rub
my palm across my face. "A woman?"

"Yes. She's pretty shaken up. I had to pay the cabbie that
dropped her off—it's obvious she's running from someone.
And I think she might need some medical attention." Max
isn't one to get ruffled by much, so hearing the concern in
the tone of his voice has me concerned.

I sit upright, kicking the sheet off my body, and press my feet
to the floor. "I'll be right down."

I shove the device into the pocket of my sweats and rush into
the elevator without stopping to put on shoes or a shirt. It's

after midnight so I don't give a fuck about my barely dressed appearance—besides, I don't know who could be in my lobby at this hour and if Max thinks she's hurt, my state of dress is of little consequence.

The elevator descends, but as soon as it stops at the lobby, I waste no time making my way over to where Max is waiting. When he sees my appearance, his eyes widen for a fraction of a second, before he quickly schools his expression and greets me halfway across the marbled floor.

"Sir." He blows out a breath and nods his head in the direction of the main entrance. "Sorry to pull you out of bed… but she insisted."

I wave my hand in the air and start to move around him in search of the late-night stranger. "It's fine. Where is *she*?"

"Should I call someone?" He turns his head, my eyes following his line of sight.

The air is knocked fully from my lungs when my gaze lands on the woman standing with her back to me. I don't need her to turn around to know precisely who she is or why she's here in my building. "No. I've got this. Thanks, Max."

I take three strides to where she stands and stop a few inches from her body. It pleases me and pains me all at the same time to see her here because I know her presence can only mean one thing—she needs my help. Pushing aside the strange feeling worming its way into my chest, I take a breath and speak the one name that could bring me to my knees.

"Rhiannon."

9

Rhiannon

THE MOMENT my husband first struck my face, I knew I needed to leave. As soon as Heath passed out, I got out. Now… standing here with *him* staring at me like he's ready to burn down the world for me, I worry I've jumped from one monster to another.

I know what I probably look like. My eyes are no doubt swollen with the tears I've shed the entire ride here, but that doesn't stop him as he reaches out and brushes the hair shielding my face. I can see the fight he is having with himself, to refrain from saying something that might trigger more tears or an even bigger breakdown. There's no hiding why I'm here… the evidence is written across my face in the form of my husband's handprint. The traitorous mark, along with the split skin in the corner of my eye, isn't something I can discount as an accident. I wasn't surprised when the cab driver didn't question why a woman with no shoes was climbing into the back of his car—he didn't need to once he got a good look at my face. He did ask if I wanted to go to the police, to which I shook my head and handed over the card I had hidden in my cast. The one Drake had given me tonight at the gala.

I hiss at the sensation of Drake's touch as he traces the tattered marks crisscrossing my skin, but I don't move away. Despite the mortification of my situation, I feel safe even just standing here with a man I barely know. It's like he gives off a pheromone that sparks the calm in my restless veins.

"He did this to you?" His voice is laced with thinly veiled anger as he continues to assess the damage Heath left behind.

I close my eyes; tears streaming down my cheek and take in an emotionally painful breath. "Yes—It's not the first time, Drake." I glance down in shame, not wanting to see the pity in his eyes.

"It'll be the last time." He turns, lacing his fingers with mine, and guides me to the elevator. "Max," he calls over his shoulder to the man that helped me inside. "No one is allowed inside the building tonight. Lock us down, please."

The elevator doors open, and Drake guides me inside. "You don't have to do all that." I finally look at him with a timid expression. "I didn't know where else to go, but I didn't mean to disrupt your night."

He spins suddenly to face me full on. He pauses, seeming to mull over his words with a look of hesitation before he speaks. "I told you I'd help you, Rhiannon. I meant what I said. You'll be safe here until we can figure out our next steps." He closes his eyes and shakes his head as he corrects himself. "*Your...* your next steps."

The doors ding, signaling our arrival on another floor. I gasp when I notice we've stopped at a massive penthouse apartment. He steps out, holding the elevator doors open and sticks his palm face up for me to take. "Come. Let's get you situated."

I take an unsteady breath and follow him into the foyer, practically tripping over myself when I realize not only is it a penthouse, but it appears to be *his* penthouse. "Isn't there somewhere else you can put me? I thought you had facilities here in the building?" I glance around at his private space, nerves coiling in my gut.

"You'll stay here, Rhiannon." He

I glance over at him, my mind finally catching up to the man standing in front of me. He's barefoot and shirtless. And *his* body differs vastly from the man I'm married to. Married… I'm a married woman in a half-naked man's apartment in the middle of the night—yet that doesn't stop my body's reaction, nor my appraisal of his muscular frame.

"I shouldn't be here." I twist my fingers together, my nerves working overtime as I scan the room, we're standing in. "I'm married. What are people going to say?"

Drake steps forward and presses his palm to my face. His thumb brushes across my cheek as he holds my gaze with his own. "When they see your face? They will say you've been trapped in a marriage that was going to get you killed. I promise, you're safe here — even from me."

He steps back, putting some needed space between us. I can't help but feel trepidation at the loss of his touch. Drake's stiff frame screams warnings at me and I find myself wondering if I've made a mistake coming to him. "Are you dangerous?"

The honesty in his voice makes my breath catch. "Yes."

I take a step back from him, fear burning in my core. "But not like your husband."

"What do you mean, *not like my husband*??

"I take what I want without a second thought—but on my terms and by my rules. But there's something about you that might have me crossing the line. I swore I wouldn't, Rhiannon. The only thing keeping me from doing something *dumb* —is your need to feel safe right now."

My heart is hammering inside my chest at his bold statement, and all I can do is nod and whisper a response. "Oh."

"Come on. I'll get you something to change into and show you where you're sleeping."

Following Drake through his apartment shouldn't feel so taboo, but it does. I mean, hell, I'm running out of fear from the man who's supposed to be my husband. Truth is, I've been nothing more than a prop for Heath for years. I was forced into marriage with him eight years ago to save my father's company. Heath Carmichael is nothing more than a pervert who gets off on young girls and controls them through violence. My dad was looking at jail time for embezzlement and the *kind* judge offered him a way out... me. The sad truth is my dad did nothing wrong. It was all a setup, and we didn't learn that until the I-dos were said and consummated.

My dad doesn't even know what kind of monster he saddled me with. If he did, it'd kill him. The mere fact I went along with this sham of a wedding surprised him, but I couldn't watch my mother fall apart for something we both knew he didn't do, so I agreed to marry Heath. All these years later, I've suffered in silence—broken bones, stitches and complete isolation from everyone, including my parents. Last week at the hospital was the first time in months that I'd seen my mother. Heath makes sure I'm kept locked up and hidden from the public eye. I believed Drake when he said he could help me. And now, I'm standing here staring at a man who evokes a myriad of feelings I don't understand.

"Here." Drake holds out a t-shirt to me. "You can use this for bed. In the morning, I'll make some calls to get you clothes. Would you like to take a shower?"

My body flushes with embarrassment for a moment, and all I can do is nod.

He places his hand on my back and ushers me into the massive bathroom attached to his bedroom. The master bathroom is huge—even bigger than the ridiculous one I left behind. He steps into the walk-in enclosure and turns on the water. I watch as he grabs a towel from the linen closet off to the side and lays it down on the vanity. "Here's a towel. Use what you need. Everything I have is yours."

I know he means his shower essentials when he says everything, he has is mine, but his words have a deeper meaning to me. This man, a man who hardly knows me, has offered me sanctuary without a second thought.

"Thank you. Um..." I glance down at my cast and close my eyes. "Do you have a trash bag I can wrap this in?" I hold out the bright pink nuisance and sigh. "I can't get it wet."

"Shit. I forgot." He spins on his heel and disappears out the door, leaving me alone with my thoughts.

I stare at the glass enclosure, lost in my own head, as I try to rationalize what I've done. Leaving is going to start a shit storm—one I've avoided for years. But the constant reminder in the form of a bright pink cast covering my arm. I know that staying with Heath is a one-way street to death. It's just a matter of time before one more hit is the last. Heath's rage has grown exponentially over the last year. Some of that rage is my fault. He wanted children, and I wasn't about to give him any, so I took precautions he didn't know about preventing them. Of course, he accused me of being damaged goods, resulting in even more of his wrath.

"Here." The touch of his hand on my back makes me jump and stumble forward. "*Fuck.*" Drake drops the plastic bag and wraps his arms around me. He tugs me against his sturdy chest like I'm an injured animal, cradling me from taking a spill. "I'm so sorry, Rhiannon. I didn't think about how walking up on you would startle you."

The sincerity in his voice is like a hammer to glass, and my insides splinter. Tears fall unabashedly and the sobs rip out of me, causing me to shake in his hold. Drake turns me around, wrapping me in an embrace with my face pressed against his chest. His hand strokes my head as he whispers against my ear. "You're safe now, little dove. He won't hurt you anymore —you have my word."

My hands cling to the bare skin of his back as my face presses against the defined ridges of muscles on his front. I can't help but notice how intimate the hold feels, which causes me to involuntarily press into him more.

Drake senses my need for a connection and tightens his hold. "What do you need, Rhiannon?"

"I don't know. Everything about this is wrong, but for the first time, I feel safe and… I don't want to let go. I know that's weird and I'm sorry to make you feel uncomfortable. But for so long, I've lived in fear and now..." my words trail off.

"Now you feel what it's like to be wanted for more than a possession." He winds his fingers into my hair, holding me in place as his fingers stroke my bare shoulder. "You belong to no one, Rhiannon. I told you earlier that whoever you're with should worship you… not control you." He pulls away, breaking the contact between us. "Let's get you cleaned up and in bed. You deserve a good night's rest and tomorrow we'll figure out how to deal with this mess."

"Thank you." I step back and retrieve the bag from the ground. Slipping my hand into the sack, Drake reaches forward and helps me secure it over my arm, so it won't get wet. I bite my lip nervously when I realize he's going to have to help me get undressed. "I hate to ask this… but can you unzip me? I can't do it with my left hand."

Drake inhales sharply, freezing for a brief second before giving me a slight nod of his head. He twirls his finger, urging me to spin and face away from him. When his fingers scarcely brush against my skin, my body pebbles with goose-bumps. He lets out a low growl, one I'm positive he was trying to stifle, as he lowers the zipper to the point just above my ass. I'm not wearing a bra beneath the fitted black dress my husband insisted I wear, and the thong I do have on does little to cover my plump backside.

His hands stay on the fabric of my dress a little longer than needed, and I almost weep when he finally pulls them off me. "I'll be in the bedroom. If you need me, holler."

With that, he bolts from the room, pulling the door slightly closed behind him. Letting the dress drop to the floor, I turn to look at myself in the mirror. There is a splattering of new and week-old bruises littering my skin that start at my hips and travel the length of my torso. Heath isn't a nice man when he demands something from me—if I try to refuse his advances, he takes it anyway… painfully.

I push down the satin thong and kick it over to where my dress pools on the floor, then step inside the glass stall. The hot water prickles against my skin, causing me to tense at the sensation. Even though my cast is covered, I make a conscious effort to keep it out of the water. Dipping my head beneath the spray, I let the water flow over my head, washing away the dirty feeling I've carried around since—well, forever.

At thirty years old, I thought I would be a mother already. But *that* dream is long forgotten. What man would want the damaged goods standing here? The baggage I carry isn't something a normal man could handle - not when they learn the sexual torment Heath put me through. I've never had an orgasm, never made love, never felt a connection to anyone sexually. For me, sex is a job. And one I *hate*. Heath wasn't my first, and I'm grateful for that. At least in my head, I know what it should be between people who are in love. What Heath and I have is anything but.

I grab Drake's bottle of shampoo and squirt some on my head. Using my good hand, I scrub the brown curls tumbling down my back and rinse. I stare at the bubbles swirling down the drain and my heart stutters. I attempt to muffle the sob that slips free by biting my fist, but the emotions overtake me. I lean against the cool tile wall and slide down to the floor on my butt. The cast now forgotten, I drag my knees to my chest and let the tears come as I press my face to the tops of my legs. This is my life now… a tangled web of fucked up lies. Lies that have me on the run from a monster whose ring I wear.

I'll never be whole again… and if even I could be, I'll be alone.

10

Drake

IT TAKES every ounce of willpower for me to turn and walk out of that goddamned bathroom. I know she thinks the growl I tried to stifle when drawing down her zipper was from pure attraction. One I made clear, and one I know she feels too, but it wasn't—not entirely. The lower the metal clasp got, the more of her bare skin I saw. Which means I saw more than enough to know I want to *murder* her husband. Her perfect alabaster skin was marred with bruises, starting at her tailbone all the way to her shoulder blades.

I shouldn't be feeling such a visceral reaction to a woman I just met, but I do, and I don't know how I'm supposed to handle that. If it were a normal day, I'd go to the club and work out my pent-up frustration. But leaving her here to take care of *my* carnal needs is not an option. Pacing the floor, I can't keep my eyes from going back to the partially opened door. She's broken and I know what that feels like. It can consume you, change you, and make you hate the world. And I don't want someone like her becoming someone like me. I will do everything I can to keep my darkness from enveloping her—no matter how strong the pull is to suck her in.

Pressing my phone to my ear, I call the only person I trust with the information that Rhiannon is here at my place.

"Drake." Archer's voice is groggy and slightly bemused at my late-night communication. "This must be important for you to be calling me at this hour. At least, it *better* be."

"It is." I scrub my hand down my face and sigh into the phone. "Judge Carmichael's wife showed up at my building this evening. He thought slapping her around tonight would keep her in line."

"*Fuck.* Did you say Judge Carmichael's wife?" I hear shuffling in the background as he's no doubt getting out of bed. "Where is she now?"

My eyes glance toward the cracked door to my bathroom and I peer into the partially obstructed view of the mirror. "My shower."

Archer clicks his tongue and grumbles something that vaguely sounds like a string of colorfully chosen words. "Did you say your *shower*? Please tell me I heard you wrong."

"Yeah—you heard me right. Look... she appeared outside the building in her ball gown from the gala and no shoes. Max got her inside after paying her cab fare and called me. I'm pretty sure the judge caused her to fall down the stairs last week, resulting in her broken arm."

"That doesn't explain why she's in your shower and not in one of the sanctuary apartments." Archer's tone bites as he practically judges me with the underlying accusation in his words.

I move toward the bathroom, taking several breaths to control the defensiveness I feel at his hidden innuendo and pause. "She will be under my personal care until I figure out how to approach this situation. I'm going to need you to place a guard at my residence until further notice."

"Jesus *Christ*, Drake." Archer grumbles something unintelligible to himself. "You and your fucking brothers certainly know how to pick them. Seriously? You run around like a goddamn statue with no feelings for years and *now* you wanna Deputy Dumbass? When have you ever taken an interest like this in a woman's wellbeing? Need I remind you she's *married* and any involvement with her can make this ten times messier - not to mention send the wrong message?"

My fist clenches the device in my hand, threatening to crack the screen in a fit of rage. "I don't give a *fuck* about the message it sends, and neither should you. If I recall, I pay you to keep things from getting messy, so do your fucking job."

Archer must hear the seriousness in my voice because he sighs through the line. "Drake... are you sure this woman is worth the tornado of shit you're about to conjure?"

My head jerks to the bathroom door when I hear the unmistakable sound of Rhiannon crying. Her sobs are loud enough to be heard over the shower, gutting me as I inch closer to the door. "I've weathered storms before for far less... I've got to go. Get a man over here by morning."

I disconnect, hesitating for a fraction of a second before I push open the barrier separating us and step through. When I do, my knees almost buckle out from under me at the sight before me. Rhiannon is on her ass, knees drawn to her chest, and crying so hard her entire body is shaking. She's so lost in her grief she doesn't react to the sound of me as I step inside.

Laying my phone on the sink, I step into the enclosure, ignoring the water soaking the fabric of my gray sweatpants and scoop her into my arms.

"I've got you." I whisper against her ear as I cradle her in my arms, wishing I could take this heartache away from her. I don't know what she's feeling exactly, but I'll never forget seeing the same pain on my mother's face.

Ignoring how her naked body feels against my bare chest, I step out of the shower. Shifting her in my arms, and being careful not to drop her, I grab the towel and drape it over her before carrying her into my room. Sitting her down on my bed, I gently towel her off. Once I'm done, I dry myself off the best I can and press my hand to her knee.

"Wait here." I wrap the cotton around her arms and hurry to retrieve the t-shirt I loaned her from the bathroom.

Rhiannon is sitting in an almost catatonic state when I return. Her brown hair is draped in front of her face, shielding her eyes as she looks at the floor. I use the discarded towel to dry her hair as best I can before pulling the shirt over her head.

I pull down the comforter and pat the mattress. "Let's get you in bed."

Her head snaps up to meet my gaze, confusion swirling in the pools of blue looking back at me. "What? I can't take your bed."

"You can... and you will. I'll sleep in the guest room." Her eyes trail the length of my body, stopping at the very prominent outline of my cock as I guide her beneath the sheet.

The wet sweatpants do little to hide my arousal from her eyes. She shifts nervously on the bed as her gaze finally comes back to mine. I pull the covers over her fragile body and give her a sincere smile.

"Try to sleep, little dove. I'll be just down the hall, but first I'm going to change out of these wet clothes." I walk to my dresser and pull out some boxer briefs. Rhiannon is facing my direction, but her gaze is vacant, almost unseeing, as she watches me. Turning my back to her, I push the wet material down, not caring that I'm commando beneath the joggers, and pull-on dry underwear. I should have used the bathroom, but a small part of me wanted to let her see.

Glancing over my shoulder, I see her eyes fixated on me. Her chest rises and falls in quick shallow breaths, almost bordering on panic. Not wanting to call attention to her reaction, I turn my head away from her probing eyes. "I'll be back in the morning."

I start toward the door, but the sound of Rhiannon whimpering my name, causes my body to seize up. "Drake." I look over my shoulder, hardly containing the need to storm to the bedside and wrap her in my arms. "Please… can you stay in here with me? I'm afraid to be alone."

My knuckles go white as I grip the edge of the wooden frame and hold my breath. The anguish in her tone makes my heart splinter in two and blow out the breath I'm holding. I turn and close the door without a word. After I turn off the light, I drag the chair I keep next to my bedside table beside her and sit down.

She sighs deeply, as though she's letting go of some of the worry she's plagued with. "Try to sleep, Rhiannon. I'll be here all night, so there's nothing for you to worry about." I pray my soothing words give her enough comfort to get some rest, even if it means *I* don't.

As her breaths even out, I focus on the outline of her still frame, and watch as she finally seems to drift off to sleep. I've never had a woman in my house, much less my bed, so this is unsettling for me in more ways than I care to admit. When I finally close my eyes after getting comfortable enough to rest in the chair, a soft whimper from Rhiannon has me jerking them wide open and sends my entire body into high alert.

Her body writhes under the sheet from what appears to be a fitful slumber. And when she lets out a soft cry into the room —I freeze. My eyes lock on the beautiful woman currently caught in what appears to be a night terror. I'm not sure if I should go to her or let her work through the terror herself. When she finally settles, I settle into the cushions and allow myself to get comfortable. Just as my eyes drift shut, the vibration of my phone causes me to fall out of the chair. I bolt upright and dive for the offending device bouncing across the top of the table and press it to my ear as I move away from the bed.

"*What?*" I bark into the phone, pissed that someone is calling me at this hour. Glancing over my shoulder, my eyes track Rhiannon's still frame and I sigh in relief when I realize it hasn't woken her up.

"I fucked up." Gage's voice fills the line and immediately my rage dissipates. "Drake… this is—I fucked up."

Groaning, I reach up with my free hand and pinch the bridge of my nose to keep myself calm as I reply quietly, "Gage. What are you talking about? The girl? You can bring her back here if you want. Stay in a sanctuary apartment if you want."

"I think Hugo knows where we are." He sighs into the phone. "There have been some weird things happening, and now

Poppy is spooked. Where are you in getting this thing finalized?"

Shaking my head, I inhale deeply to try to tamp down the irritation threatening to creep into my voice. "Fuck, Gage... I just filed last week. Hugo paid me a visit and I can tell you this will not be easy. Call Archer. Tell him what's going on and let him assess the situation."

"Fine." He breathes out a heavy breath in frustration. "I'm sorry Drake. I didn't mean to cause problems like this... but this woman—" his words die on his tongue, and I find myself glancing back at the one currently in my bed.

A sigh of own slips out of my mouth as I admit, "I think I get it, Gage. Just... be careful. Ok? Your life is more important than a woman you barely know, and Hugo isn't someone to fuck with."

"My life means nothing anymore... we were wrong, Drake. *So,* fucking wrong." I hear the soft murmur of someone in the background. "I gotta go. I'll call Archer."

I stare at my cell phone when the line goes dead. A heavy feeling weighs in the pit of my stomach because of his words —*we were wrong.* I don't want to admit I know what he was talking about, but as I turn to find a pair of weary eyes watching me in the dark... everything I thought I believed comes crashing down around me.

She watches as I stalk toward the bedside and lay my cell phone down, this time silencing it completely. My eyes flick between her and the chair briefly before I give in and walk around to the opposite side of the bed. Tugging the covers down, I slip in beneath them without a word and close my eyes. I don't care what implications having her in my bed means — I'm done fighting the need to be close to her.

I'll free her from the monster who's spent a decade tormenting her, even if it means showing her the darkness inside me. I can be exactly what she needs, even if it's not what she wants. I just hope it doesn't scare her off. Because lying here beside her, listening to the sounds of her breathing... I know I'm close to crossing a line I won't be able to redraw.

I can be as ruthless as necessary when it comes to protecting a woman. It's something I've built my life around since watching my mother die at the hands of the man she trusted implicitly. A man that was supposed to love and protect not just her, but my brothers and me. If it hadn't been for my aunt showing us how family *really* looked and behaved, we'd have all turned out just like him—evil. It's one of the many reasons I've kept myself corded off from emotional entanglements. Until this very moment, I've never felt the urge to break down the barriers around my soul for anyone... and that thought has me scared shitless.

With my head heavy, I finally close my eyes and give into sleep. The morning is going to bring a firestorm our way.

I'm going to need to be on my game to make this work—or we could both lose it *all*.

11

Rhiannon

I FEEL like I've been in a car accident. My entire body is stiff and aches with a tightness I know is from the beating I took last night. It was the final straw, driving me out of my home in the middle of the night, barefoot—and straight to a complete stranger. Which is how I wound up currently pressed against a man I hardly know.

Taking stock of my current position, I close my eyes and inhale the unmistakably spicy scent of men's body wash. It's a smell that will be burned into my memory forever because it brings a sense of calm over me, I've never known. I *should* be ashamed for flinging myself into the arms of another man, but there's something about Drake that makes me feel safe— even with his arm wrapped tightly around me like a vise, it's the first time I've felt anything other than trapped in the arms of a man.

My leg is draped over his lower half, precariously pressed against the morning wood beneath his boxers. He obviously climbed into the bed last night wearing only his underwear, because the rest of my body is currently glued to his bare chest, with my face nestled in the crook of his shoulder. This is not a familiar position for me, as Heath and I rarely slept in the same bed. Once he got what he needed, usually by force, he would go to his study.

"This is an interesting turn of events." Drake's deep voice rasps, sending shivers all the way to my toes. "Rhiannon, I'm not sure how we ended up like this, but I think you should move."

His words are like a dagger to my heart, so I suck in a breath and roll away from him. Drake must sense my hurt, because he moves faster than I expect, pinning me beneath his body. "Stop." His voice commands me as he peers down at me, his face a mask of turmoil and regret.

"I'm sorry. I... I didn't mean to make you uncomfortable." I stutter my response, embarrassed by my body's reaction.

Drake furrows his brows at my words. "*Uncomfortable?*" He shifts, so he's wedged between my legs, only thin cotton separating us. "Rhiannon, the only thing that's uncomfortable is the fucking hard-on I have right now." He presses himself against my center, showing me what he means. "But you're not mine, and this can't happen right now."

He flings himself off me and stands beside the bed. "I need to make some calls. I'm certain your husband will be looking for you. He's likely already called the police, and we need to get out ahead of this—*fast*." He turns and starts toward the bathroom. Pausing at the entrance, he glances over his shoulder. "But make no mistake, Rhiannon... I want you."

Drake steps inside the bathroom and I hear the shower kick on. A part of me wants to be reckless - wants to see what being desired by a complete stranger feels like, because all I've known for the last decade is control and demand. I can't even recall what the men I'd been with before Heath were like. Maybe that makes me broken, but I can honestly say I've never felt an attraction like this to anyone. Climbing from the bed, I tiptoe my way over to the open door and lean against the frame. I can see around the door's edge and into the shower stall, making me feel like some kind of peeping Tom.

Holding my breath as I bite down on my lip, I watch as Drake sheds his boxers and steps into the glass enclosure. His body is a work of art, right down to his perfectly sculpted backside. He steps beneath the spray of water facing away from me. I can't take my eyes off the way the water drips down his muscular back, down his legs, and swirls into the drain. My breath hitches slightly when he grabs the soap and lathers his body up, suds covering every square inch. And when he turns to rinse them from his skin, my eyes don't miss the erection he's sporting. The same erection he pressed between my legs moments ago. His cock is unlike anything I've seen. Sure, I'd been with men before Heath - *two,* to be exact. But they were young, average, run-of-the-mill, college guys who could never give me an orgasm. And Heath... well, he lacks in that department as well. Sex with him was always savage in some fashion, and I've never climaxed—which usually makes him furious with me and led to another beating.

Looking at Drake's cock, my insides clench with a foreign sensation. I haven't come from something that wasn't of my own doing, and even that hasn't been in years. I turn to leave, embarrassed by my own visceral reaction to this man, but my name spills from his lips before I can walk away.

"Rhiannon."

I close my eyes, thinking he's caught me, but what I see when I open them has me gasping for air. Drake's eyes are closed as one hand is braced against the tiled wall. The other is wrapped around his shaft in a firm grip. His body is tense and the muscles in his arm begin to flex as he strokes his palm along his cock. His movements become tremulous as he increases the speed, hungry for a release. I watch in complete fascination as he explodes, crying out my name once more.

"Rhiannon."

His cum spurts out like a volcano erupting, but he doesn't stop—he continues pulling at himself until he's spent every drop onto the tiled floor. Even as he lets his dick go, my eyes widen when I see it's still semi-hard, something I didn't think was possible. I trail my eyes up his body and freeze. Drake is staring at me through heated eyes. I expect to see anger, but what I see has me shocked to the core. His eyes are hooded as he licks his lips and smirks. He rubs his palm over himself again, letting the mushroom head bob against his belly. The entire time, his eyes haven't left mine.

I turn away and press myself against the wall, mortified I've been caught. What the fuck am I doing? I came here fleeing a broken marriage, only to lust after another man. A man who, by all accounts including his own, is supposedly a player— I've heard the rumors about how he doesn't do attachments. How he's a billionaire playboy that uses women for sex… and I refuse to be used again. I'm here to get free of the man who's stolen my life from me, not wind up as a toy for another. Even as I walk away from the door, I know the need to feel something more from a man like him is dangerous. Yet, I can't shake the allure.

"Rhiannon." Drake calls my name from behind me. "Turn around, little dove." I pause but refuse to do as he commands.

"I can't," I whisper, ashamed. "I shouldn't have invaded your privacy like that. I don't know what possessed me to do it, but it won't happen again."

The heat of his body pressed up behind me startles me. "Oh, it'll happen again. I told you—you're not mine *yet*, Rhiannon. But you will be." He grips my shoulders and spins me to face him. "Did you like what you saw?"

"I..." I swallow hard, holding his gaze as he appraises me with a knowing grin. I don't have to answer him for the truth to be revealed—it's written all over my face.

"Tell me the truth, Rhi. There's nothing to be ashamed of."

"I'm married—" He silences me with his lips on mine. At first, fear takes hold and I back away, but Drake presses his hand to my back, slowly tracing his fingers over the shirt I'm wearing, and I give in. This isn't a kiss I'm familiar with. It's demanding, but not in a forcible way. He has yet to push his tongue inside my mouth and instead he sucks my bottom lip between his teeth, biting down.

He pulls back, his hand still nestled in the curve of my spine. "You *are* married—and I've always made it a point not to involve myself with a client or a married woman. And I've never had a woman in my apartment, nor my bed. But you..." He rubs his thumb over my swollen lip. "...have destroyed every rule I've made for myself."

"Rules? I don't understand."

He winds his fingers into my mussed hair. "I can help you break the ties from the villain you're married to but being with a man like me comes with its own cost."

I blink back the tears at the reality of my situation. "I'll pay whatever I need to be free of him."

"Not money, little dove." He tugs my hair, tilting my head back to expose my neck. "There are two kinds of monsters—the one that torments and fill you with fear."

I whisper as his lips press against my ear, the heat of his breath prickling my skin. "And the other?"

"The kind that consumes your soul, burning anyone and anything that threatens to take his most prized possession."

My eyes close in ecstasy as he touches his lips to my neck. "Which one are you?"

"Both." He steps back, leaving me cold and confused. "I'm not the person you deserve, Rhiannon. Darkness pollutes my veins. Which is why wanting you is so dangerous. You deserve a man—not a monster."

"You're not a monster, Drake." I take a step toward him but stop. "A monster wouldn't open his door to a woman he barely knows in the wee hours of the night. He wouldn't scoop her up from the shower floor where she sits broken and lost—-then care for her. And he certainly wouldn't warn her of the dangers a man like him carries."

"You don't know what you're talking about, little dove." He shakes his head and sighs. "You've endured years of abuse. You don't know what normal love is, and that's not something I can show you because I've never experienced normal love, either. Plus, I have needs you can't and won't be able to understand. Things I wouldn't dare show you because of the hell you've lived. And that alone is why this—" he waggles his finger between us, "...can't happen."

"Can't or *won't?*" I take a step toward him. "Because from what I saw in there..." I point toward the bathroom. "...you want me."

"Yes. I won't deny that Rhiannon. But you need time to heal. Time to decide what you want. I watched my mother give in to the hands of my father, who was the definition of evil. I won't be him. You will always have a choice, Rhiannon."

Swallowing hard, I admit, "That's more than I get with Heath."

"What?" Drake's body stiffens at my statement.

I clear my throat and try to bolster my voice, so I don't sound weak. "A choice. I was forced into the marriage under lies. And the control didn't stop there. He has always used sex as a punishment and taken away my freedoms. I'm a thirty-year-old woman who should be in a classroom of students, yet I've never been allowed to have anything for myself."

"You deserve to have that—to have everything you want." He turns and tugs open his dresser drawer to pull out a pair of boxers. "Sex should be used to fulfill fantasies, desires—leave you breathless. The mere fact you've had to experience it the way you describe, is even more reason I won't touch you."

I push my fingers through my hair in frustration and growl. "Shouldn't I get a say in what I want or need?"

He drops the towel and tugs on his boxers, my eyes trailing the firm backside as his muscles flex beneath the material. "I crave things you couldn't possibly handle, Rhiannon. Sex is my way of burying the demons inside me. Physical pleasure keeps the monster my father branded me with sedated, so I don't turn into him. That's not how sex should be for you —ever."

I don't mean to sound so childish, but I'm tired of being told what I can handle or do and the little stamp from my foot is almost involuntary. "I don't know what I can deal with. I've never been given a chance to decide. And taking that away from me makes you no better than *him*."

He looks over his shoulder at me, his eyes boring into mine. He stalks toward me, his hand curling around my neck. I gasp, shocked at the show of dominance as the wall bites into my back. "And you think you could handle being held down and fucked?" His fingers tighten, slightly cutting off the air to my lungs. "Or having your body bent at *my* complete mercy while you're brought close to release, then denied? Because that's what I like... what I crave. My sexual appetite comes with a safe word, little dove."

His fingers loosen, and I take a much-needed breath as tears prickle in my eyes. "Is it to humiliate the woman? Is that why you do those things?"

There's a flash of darkness that crosses his face as his eyes narrow. "No. It's about control. Something I didn't have when my father *murdered* my mother."

I don't stifle the gasp of horror at his admission. "Sounds like you're just as broken as me."

"Perhaps that's true." He steps back. "Get dressed. Feel free to go through my drawers and find something temporary. Someone will be bringing you clothes later."

12

Drake

As EXPECTED, my phone hasn't stopped ringing. Rhiannon has been in my care for two weeks and it's been one fucking thing after another. Not to mention the torture it's been trying *not* to cross the line with her when my body craves her like a drug. Her husband has threatened to have me arrested, my business destroyed, and my favorite—me disbarred. None of which is possible.

First, it was Archer, giving me an update on Gage's situation. They've doubled the men around his place since there's evidence Hugo has men stationed in the town. How they even know where he is has me furious with the reality that someone in our midst is likely a rat.

I press the speaker button on my desk phone and dial Judge Whitaker's number. He's helped expedite things for me in the past, with a little monetary encouragement, so I hope he'll be as willing this time.

"Whitaker." He barks into the line.

"Judge. It's Drake Winston." I pause, waiting for the irritated reaction I know is coming.

His sigh through the phone tells me he knows my call isn't something pleasant. "What do you need, Drake? You're not on my docket, so I know this isn't about a case."

I tap the pen I'm holding on the desktop. "I need your help to expedite a protection order case that is set for next month."

"It must be serious if you can't wait thirty days."

I lean back in my chair and close my eyes. "It is, and you won't like it, so we can get that out of the way, but I need this pushed through."

He sighs on the other end of the line. "Fine. Who is it? I'll see if I can squeeze it onto my docket for next week."

"Alessandro Hugo."

"Fuck no," he grunts into the phone. "I'm not touching that—why the *fuck* are you involved with anything related to that man? Do you know the shitstorm I'll have to deal with if I hear that case in my courtroom?"

I blow out a frustrated breath. "What will it take? I have a personal interest in this cluster fuck."

His silence grates my nerves, but I know this case will bring a heavy cloud over him and his family. Especially when Hugo *doesn't* win. "Two-hundred thousand."

"How about three? Just to, you know, ensure things are handled promptly? I'll take care of the transfer so it's not traceable to me. Looks like you just came into some family money, Judge. Send me the updated date, as well as his attorney."

The uptick in the judge's voice is minimal as he clears his throat. "I hope you know what you're doing, Winston. Between this and Judge Carmichael's wife going missing, I don't know how much more stress I can take."

"She's not missing," I grumble into the line. "In fact, for the first time in years, she's perfectly safe… depending on your definition of the word, at least."

Whitaker coughs into the line as I imagine he must've just sat straight up in whatever seat he's occupying. "Please tell me you're not involved in this, too?"

Laughing sourly, I reply without missing a beat, "She's here under my protection while we start the proceedings for her divorce."

Whitaker's voice sounds like he's on the verge of wheezing. "Please tell me you're messing with me, Drake. You know it's not even April, so this isn't funny. For the love of God, tell me you're not the reason he's taken a leave of absence to sort out their marriage. I just assumed it was typical marital problems, not another man."

Tapping my pen on the desk with a huff, I respond, "I'm not kidding. Rhiannon Carmichael is here with me and has been for two weeks. But it's not what you're assuming, rest assured. She's desperate to get away from that monster, and I aim to help her do just that. He broke her arm, nearly killing her when he shoved her down the steps of their home."

I nearly laugh when I hear the sharp intake of breath on the other line and drive home my point, "Did you know that was the type of man he is, or did you really believe that whole bullshit about her falling down the stairs and bruising her face and back of her head in the process? I mean, really, how does one get bruises in the shape of fingerprints on *accident*?

He beat her—regularly. Is that who you want trying cases beside you?"

"I... I didn't know. I've suspected he wasn't who we thought, but beating a woman? I'll help you with that however I can." His silence tells me he's thinking about a man who is supposed to uphold the law, not break it, sitting on the bench in the same courtroom as him. "I don't tolerate a man using his position to control anyone like that."

I smile at his response. Even though he can be bought for some things, Whitaker at heart is a good man. "Good. I'll be in touch with you as soon as we've sorted out the evidence and details."

I press the button, ending the call with the judge, and lean back in my chair. As I do, I'm surprised to find Rhiannon standing in my office doorway. She's wearing a sundress, one of many items my assistant bought for her. My assistant did a damn fine job because everything she bought Rhiannon fit her like a glove. This dress in particular does little to hide the perfectly sized breasts thinly veiled beneath the semitransparent fabric.

"What are you doing here?" I arch a brow at her as she steps inside and tugs the door closed behind her.

She twists her fingers in front of her, something I notice she does when she's nervous. "Is it true?"

"Is what true?" I spin the pen I'm holding between my fingers as I watch her.

Her voice is timid as she continues to fidget with her hands, all while holding my gaze. "That he's taken a leave of absence to hunt me down?"

"Yes. But I'm taking care of it—I promised you're safe here. I meant it, Rhiannon." I push up from my seat and make my way around the desk. I'm inches from her, and I can see the fear in her eyes. "He will not hurt you again."

"What about you?" She glances up, her eyes filled with worry.

Our faces are so close that I can feel the heat of her breath on my skin. "What about me?"

"Are *you* going to hurt me?" She glances down at her feet, seemingly embarrassed by the question.

Pressing my finger beneath her chin, I slowly raise her eyes to meet mine. I stare into the depths of her cerulean eyes and see what I've refused to accept for my entire life—hope. There's a connection burning between us - one that doesn't care about the current situation or the hell we are about to deal with.

And that leads me to do what I promised myself I wouldn't. "I'm going to kiss you, Rhiannon. And if that isn't something you want right now, pull away and walk out while you still can."

I hold my breath, part of me praying she walks out of my office and the other silently begging her to stay. When she leans in, her eyes daring me to make good on my promise, I lose all sense of control and fit my mouth over hers. Her lips are soft beneath mine and I can sense the slight unease in her movements, but I don't let it stop or slow me down. I fist her hair in my hand, bending her neck to gain better access. I don't even realize I'm backing her up until her body hits the closed door. This is wrong on so many levels. The first being she's still a married woman—and to a judge, no less. But it doesn't stop me from pressing my leg between her thighs and leaning into her body.

The heavy weight of her cast rests against my side as I deepen the kiss, my tongue darting between her lips. It's obvious to me she hasn't been kissed like this in a long time —if ever. And that calls to my inner beast like a siren on the sea.

The sound of my phone ringing snaps me from the heated exchange, reality crashing down around me like ice cold water. I step back, ripping myself away from the warmth of her soft curves, and turn on my heel to snatch the offending device from its cradle on my desk.

"What?" My eyes bore into hers, the turbulent sea-blue eyes watching me with so many questions buried inside. "You're fucking kidding me. No. I said *no*." Rhiannon moves toward me, her eyes burning a hole in my chest with each step. "Fine. I'll have her make contact."

The phone nearly snaps in two as I slam it back down onto my desk. I shove my hand through my hair and blow out a frustrated breath.

"What is it?" Rhiannon pauses, inches from me, and I can see the want in her expression.

My jaw grinds in consternation. "Your husband has learned of your location and is demanding to speak with you."

"No." She closes her eyes, shaking her head frantically. "He'll make me go back with him. I can't... please. He'll kill me if I do."

I press my palm to her cheek, my thumb tracing along the line of her lip. "He will not touch you." I lean forward and press my mouth to hers. It's a chaste kiss, but the tenderness behind it is all that matters. "I promise to set you free, little dove. Another may own you again... but you'll never be trapped in a cage."

She sucks in a breath at my promise, her pupils dilating at my words. "What do you mean? Heath owned me... I won't let that happen again."

"Oh, Rhiannon. Heath owned your mind... that's not what I'm talking about or something I would ever want."

She holds my gaze, her will stronger than I give her credit for. "What do you want?"

"More than you can handle right now. I told you—I might not be Heath, but I have demons of my own and a darkness I'm not sure you'll survive."

Her voice is low, barely a whisper, and I see the tears pooling in her eyes. "I've lived in hell for the last decade... no one knows darkness like me."

A knock at my door makes Rhiannon step away from me. Her arms fold across her chest, and I can see trepidation in her features.

"Wait here." I motion to the couch against the wall, out of sight of the door. Once she's seated and out of view for whomever is standing on the opposite side, I pull it open slightly, before tugging it wide to let in the visitor.

Archer strolls in, his body tight with unease. "We need to talk." He scans the room, his whole body freezing when his gaze lands on Rhiannon. "Holy *shit*." He blinks as if unsure of what he's seeing and slowly inches in her direction. "Rhi?"

His head swivels between me and her. "Drake... I—" Archer stops and takes a breath. I've never seen him lost for words, so his reaction has me on edge, especially when he moves to stand in front of her. She's staring at him wide-eyed, like she's seen a ghost when he reaches out and brushes his thumb across her cheek. "When you told me the judge's wife was Rhiannon Carmichael, I didn't put two and two together."

I watch in shock as Rhiannon flings her arms around one of the few men I trust with my life—and despite that fact, I can't stop the growl that bubbles out. Rhiannon begins to sob, her body shaking against his as he wraps his arms firmly around her.

"*Archer*. What the fuck?" I step beside them, yanking her from his grasp and crushing her body into mine.

"Drake. Rhiannon was one of my closest friends in high school and then in college. I didn't know it was *her* when you told me—I should have put two and two together. Had I, I would've come sooner." He takes a deep breath and sighs. "But the shit with your brother has kept me busy." He looks down at her. "Rhi… What *happened* to you? You were there senior year of college and then suddenly gone. I knew you got married or something, but that's it. One day I had my best friend, and the next she was just gone without a word."

She nestles into my side, giving me the sense of comfort, I need. "My dad got into some trouble, and I agreed to marry the judge to keep him out of jail. It wasn't until afterwards that I learned it had all been a lie. By then it was too late, and I was the princess trapped in the tower—doomed to a life of hell."

"How did you get out now?" Archer watches my hand as it strokes her back. I can see the question in his gaze, but he doesn't dare ask.

"Drake. He gave me a way to escape and at first, I thought he was crazy... then Heath nearly killed me the night of the Gala. I used the card Drake slipped me and came here. I've been here since."

"Jesus Christ." Archer runs his palm through his hair and sighs. "Alright... Well, this makes things different. I was coming here to tell you to take her home to avoid a press scandal, but now—*fuck it*. Do whatever you can to keep her safe, Drake. Seriously. She was one of the best people I knew back then."

"I plan to, Archer. But let's get one thing straight." I hug her against me. "Rhiannon is off-limits."

He snorts, shaking his head like I've just grown a second one of my own. "Drake... I can't believe you haven't figured this out—but Rhiannon isn't my type."

I stare at him not sure I understand. "Not your type?"

"Nope... she doesn't have the right parts... but you—" he winks and turns toward her with a grin. "Shit, I've worked for Drake and his brothers for—going on nine years. You'd think he would know seeing *him* naked would do more for me than seeing *you* naked."

"Are you shitting me?" My eyes practically bulge out of my head at his admission. "How did I not know this?"

Archer raises a brow at me, daring me to make this more. "Would it matter?"

"Hell, no. You're a crazy motherfucker, Archer. I trust you with my life, and now hers." I shake my head, still shocked that I'd missed the signs someone I considered a close friend, is gay.

"Good. I'm going to go figure out how to do damage control. You should probably figure out a statement, because the press is going to be on you like flies on shit, my friend. I'll also get a status update on Gage. His mess *might* still be worse than yours, but this is going to be a shitshow all on its own." Archer hugs Rhiannon goodbye and makes his way out of my office.

But before he can get totally out, I stop him. "Archer. Can you come keep Rhiannon company tonight? I need to take care of something and don't want to leave her alone."

"Sure." He frowns, narrowing his eyes at me. "Everything okay?"

As much as I don't want to leave Rhiannon, I need to get rid of some of this pent-up frustration before I make a mistake and cross boundaries with her. "Yes. Fine. I just need to let off some steam, so I'm going to the club."

"Right... I see. Sure, I'll be up around nine." Archer shrugs, but I don't miss the disappointment in his stare as he hurries out, slamming the door behind him.

"The *club?*" Rhiannon cuts her eyes toward me, confusion marring her face.

I reach out to brush the hair out of her face, but she steps back. "I told you I have needs that I will not subject you to right now. This is the only way I can remain in control around you, little dove."

"So what? You're going to pick up a woman tonight?" Rhiannon blinks back the tears that threaten to fall. "Never mind. You don't owe me an explanation." She turns on her heel and storms out, leaving me to stare at the empty door as it slams shut.

I drop into my chair and blow out the breath I didn't realize I was holding. "Fuck."

I didn't mean to hurt her… but I can't possibly subject her to the cravings I have.

Not now… maybe never.

13

Rhiannon

"So, tell me, Rhi, what happened after graduation?" Archer is leaning against the wall watching me with curiosity. "You just —disappeared."

I huff out a deep breath and shrug. "Heath happened. My dad got into some trouble with his company, and Judge Carmichael offered him a solution. Unfortunately, that solution was *me*."

He shakes his head and purses his lips, "Has Heath—" he stops, unsure if he should ask me whatever it is on his tongue.

"Go ahead, Archer, ask me." I roll my eyes at him. He's in security, so I know he's wondering if there's been sexual abuse—and I don't know how to tell him there has.

"Rhi... *what* has he done to you? If we're going to get you out of this marriage, I need to know everything. If it's too much for you to tell me, because I'm a guy—I'll get my associate to come talk with you." His expression softens as he leans in and waits.

Archer had been one of my closest friends—but Heath took everyone out of my life that could pose a threat to him and our marriage. And Archer was one of the biggest in his mind, even though he was gay. His six-foot-three build, and shaggy blonde hair make all the girls swoon, leading to their heart-break when they realize he bats for the other team. I've never seen him sexually–even before I knew he was gay. Besides, the only man polluting my thoughts in an unladylike way is Drake.

"You're my friend Archer—at least, you used to be. It's not too much to share, but you'll look at me differently." I confess to him, knowing no matter what he thinks, the life I lived with Heath would make anyone look at me differently.

Archer stalks across the room and sits across from me on the smaller sofa. "No... I won't. What happened to you isn't your fault and I only ask because the more details I can get for Drake, the easier it will be to get you free of Heath."

"Drake needs to know the details?" My brows furrow in the realization that he's going to see just how broken I truly am, and a momentary blast of panic hits me.

"Yes. He'll need to present it to the judge when it gets to that point. I've already subpoenaed your medical records with the papers Drake had you sign." Archer narrows his eyes at me, and I know he's reading more in my question than I want him to.

Drake gave me a stack of paperwork this morning, all of which he said granted him permission to access my personal files. "I..."

Archer reaches across the table and presses his palm to my knee. "Hey... Drake is used to this kind of thing." I raise my eyes to meet him, unsure how to explain what I'm feeling.

"Oh." He smiles as he pats my leg. "You don't want him to know the details because you don't want him to see you as broken."

"I know it's crazy, Archer. I barely know him, and I shouldn't have these feelings for a man I just met, especially when I'm still married to one that nearly killed me... but something about him has me all twisted up inside. Him knowing the shit Heath put me through might—"

"Turn him off?" Archer finishes for me. "I seriously doubt a man like Drake would think any less of you because of something another man did to you, Rhi. Besides, he has his own demons."

Hearing him say that reminds me of his absence and where he has gone. "He's at a sex club, isn't he?"

"Rhi..." Archer palms the back of his neck and sighs. "Drake keeps his private life—private. If you want to know about that side of him, ask him."

Frowning, I press for information, "Why does he go there? Drake could have any woman he wants. I'm not naïve, Archer. I know there are places here in the city that cater to that sort of thing."

Archer shakes his head like this is a conversation he doesn't want to have, though he does humor me with *some* information. "His life was founded on death and destruction. He witnessed his father murder his mother when he was just a kid. And then he stood by and watched as his older brother pulled the trigger to end the devil's reign. Drake refuses to let any woman close because he believes he's just like his dad because of a few kinks he might have."

"Kinks?" I blink in confusion. "You mean like *sexual* kinks?"

"I've probably already told you too much and I *like* my job with him, Rhi." Archer fishes his phone out of his pocket and frowns. "Hold that thought a minute."

I watch as he gets up and moves to the kitchen to take his call. All the while, my mind is stuck on his words *'he believes he's just like his dad because of a few kinks he might have'*. Does he think I'm too fragile because of the life I live right now? He has no idea the things I've craved for years. The things I've wanted to feel from a man that loved me and would make it about being together, not about control.

"I don't give a fuck, Gage." Archer's raised voice pulls my attention toward the kitchen. He's pacing the floor like a cat on a hot tin roof, and I can tell he's tense by the muscles bulging in his neck. "Fine. I'll take care of it." He pockets the phone and blows out a breath. When he returns to the living room, he wears a look of pure frustration.

I tilt my head, studying his body language. "Everything okay?"

"No." He plops down on the couch. "The Winston men like to do things the *hard* way, it seems."

I curl my feet beneath my ass and reach for my drink sitting on the table. "What does that mean?"

"Drake and his brothers have always just pushed women away because it was easy. But now..." He smiles, letting his voice trail off with the unsaid words.

"Now?" I shake my head and blink at him.

"Now it seems they've all found one that's cracking through that brick wall they've built around their hearts. Shame I couldn't convince them to try me." He waggles his eyebrows at me, making me laugh. "I just hope you're ready, Rhi.

Because Drake is not an easy man. He'd never hurt you—on purpose. But it's going to take a strong woman to love him. And I don't know if you're ready for that. Not with everything you've been through."

I roll my eyes at Archer with a sigh. "I've been beaten by a man who wanted to control me and keep me under his thumb. That's not love, and I know that. I didn't leave sooner because I was ashamed, not weak. Don't confuse the two, Archer. I shouldn't want a man when I'm in the process of trying to flee one. And sure... maybe it's some kind of savior attraction because he's giving me a chance to be free—something I haven't believed I could have in a long time."

"I don't think that's it, Rhi. I think you see something in him he doesn't see in himself."

Frowning like a petulant child, I cross my arms, "And what's that?"

"Hope." Archer stands and moves toward the door. "Look, I've got to step outside and handle this mess with Gage. I'll be right outside the door if you need me."

I narrow my eyes at him and make a motion with my hand. "It's fine. I'm going to go take a bath and then head to bed. Sitting around thinking about where Drake has gotten off to is driving me nuts. Not to mention the fact I have to face Heath in the morning."

Archer lets himself out the apartment door, and I amble my way to the bathroom. Drake's apartment definitely has its perks, with the tub being one of them. It's large enough for two people to soak comfortably together. Stripping off my clothes, I turn on the faucet and heat the water up. I find some bath salts and dump them into the water, swirling them around with my foot as I slip beneath the surface, careful not to wet my cast. I stare at the bright pink fiberglass and laugh to myself. The color drove Heath mad with rage because it was unbecoming of a man like him to have his wife wear it around. *That* defiance came with the cost of bruised ribs.

Leaning my head back onto the edge of the tub, I close my eyes and let the heat of the water soothe my sore body. My thoughts immediately conjure up the image of Drake in the shower, and my body tightens with the memory. Watching him wrap his fingers around his cock made my core pulse with desire. And when he cried out my name as his cum covered the tiled wall, I thought I would explode right there on the spot.

Just thinking about his dick and the beauty of it has me slipping my hand beneath the water and between my legs. I press my finger to my clit, already swollen with desire, and hiss at the sensation as I apply pressure. This is the only way I've ever reached climax, so getting myself off isn't something new.

I visualize Drake's shaft slipping between my folds as I slide my finger inside. My back arches, splashing water onto the floor as my feet press firmly against the tiled wall. I pump my hand, inserting an additional digit to create more friction inside my core.

"Oh..." I moan out into the empty room, pressing the heel of my palm against my nub. Rubbing it around with slight pressure as I finger myself, I feel the tingling of my release building. My legs lock as I pick up speed, water splashing with each twist of my hand. I'm ready to explode when a noise causes me to open my eyes. My entire body stills at the sight before me.

"Don't stop on my account." Drake's voice is husky as he watches me from his place, standing in the doorway. His hand rubbing over the obvious arousal behind his zipper. "I was rather enjoying what you were doing, little dove."

I don't move and I'm certain I can't breathe. Drake slowly creeps toward me and drops to his knees beside the bathtub. "You didn't finish," he murmurs, his eyes moving down the arm that disappears beneath the water.

"I—" I lick my lips, unsure what to say or do. I should be embarrassed, but ironically, I'm not.

Drake strips off his jacket and rolls up his sleeve. Never taking his eyes off mine, his fingers wrap around the arm I have buried between my thighs. He pauses, waiting for me to tell him to stop, I'm sure, but I don't—I *can't*.

His palm scorches my skin despite the water as he brushes down it, disappearing into the water and between my legs. He spreads his fingers and curls them around my hand, slipping his fingers into my pussy along with mine.

His eyes close as he hisses. "*Fuck*." And for a moment, neither of us speaks or moves. It isn't until I flex my hips, pushing into his hand, that his eyes snap open and pierce me with a look of longing. It's like a trigger to a bomb because Drake pumps his hand inside me with absolute fervor. He pushes my hand out of the way, taking complete control of my pleasure. Holding gazes, he pumps harder and faster, water wetting his clothes as he does.

"Does this feel nice, little dove?" He flicks his thumb over my clit, pressing down as he curves his fingers inside me. "Does it make you want to scream in ecstasy?"

"*Please,*" I whimper, needing him to give me back the release I was so close to moments ago. I want to feel the euphoric sensation as my body lets go and sends me over the edge into oblivion—something I haven't felt in eons.

He applies more pressure, adding a third finger to the fray, triggering the most powerful orgasm I've had in a long time… if ever. I arch my back just as his lips claim my scream and swallow my cry, devouring my mouth with his.

Ripping his face from mine, Drake scoops his free hand beneath my ass, his fingers slipping free from my channel. In one quick movement, he lifts me from the tub, pressing me against his chest. His lips find mine in a fury as he stands holding me in his arms and turns towards the bedroom.

"I'm done fighting this," he mumbles against my lips, leaving a trail of water in our wake as we cross the floor. I should be scared of the feral look he has in his eyes, because I know I've just crossed a line I can never redraw.

But all I feel is relief.

Drake

I SPENT ALMOST an hour at the club trying to convince myself to take someone into a private room. Even Kat showed up and I turned her down. Something about sex with a stranger made me feel like I was betraying Rhiannon. Which is how I wound up right here, watching her masturbate in the bathtub. I didn't mean to move, startling her and causing her to freeze like a deer caught in headlights. But when she moaned and her body tensed, I lost all sense of control.

And when she willingly let me shove my hand between her legs, my cock damn near exploded inside my pants. I don't give a shit about the water covering my pristine floor, nor do I care that the eight-hundred-dollar suit pants and dress shirt I'm wearing are soaked through. Because right now, I've got the woman who has consumed my thoughts naked in my arms as I carry her to the bed.

I drop her wet frame onto the mattress and step back to appraise her body. She covers herself with one arm, but I lean forward and swat it away. "Don't. Let me see you."

Her body might be marked with faded bruises, but it doesn't detract from the sheer beauty she possesses. I hold her gaze as I strip off my now see-through shirt and toss it to the floor. Her eyes follow my hand as I unsnap my trousers and shove them down, taking the damp boxers with them. The sharp intake of breath sends a pulse of need straight to my cock, making it bob against my abdomen. I fist my shaft, giving it a slow stroke as I step toward the bed.

"I've fought this pull, Rhiannon—but I'm done." I shove her legs apart using my knee and climb between them, bracing myself above her. My dick rests against the apex of her legs that are spread open around me. "I tried to erase you from my veins tonight, but I couldn't even *look* at another woman. I'm not a good man, and you deserve someone who can give you something normal. I should let you go—but I can't." I nudge the head of my shaft between her folds, slowly burying myself inside her. Rhiannon's eyes widen with the shock I've just claimed her, but she doesn't object.

"If this becomes too much, I need you to use a safe word, Rhiannon. Do you understand? I need you to tell me you do, or this is over before it's started."

"I understand." She wiggles against me, her voice only just a whisper.

I continue trailing my fingers along the curve of her backside. "I need you to say it."

"I promise… I'll say red. That's what you mean, right?"

I nod. As innocent as it may be, it's all I need to allow myself to continue. Lacing my fingers with her hands, I pin her arms above her head and ease out, only to thrust inside her again.

"I shouldn't want you... a man like me will ruin you even more than the monster you're trying to escape." I pump my hips into her and still myself when she wraps her legs around me. "I meant to set you free, little dove." I press a heated kiss to her neck, our bodies moving in tandem. "But I can't let you go. Not now... now that I've seen what the promised land has to offer. You're like heaven and hell all rolled into one, twisting the fragments of my soul into something that resembles hope."

I drag my tongue down her throat, leaning in to suck at the flesh beneath her chin. She moans a throaty sound as her back arches off the bed, causing my cock to slip deeper inside her.

"Oh, *God*." She hisses as I continue to plunge inside her, licking my way down to her breast, where I suck a nipple between my lips. Her hands break free of my hold and latch onto my head, tugging at my hair as she pushes her hips into each thrust.

"You feel so good. Better than I could have dreamed." I lean up, sitting back on my heels, causing my shaft to slip out of her channel. Gripping her ankles, I drag her so that her core is pressed against my lap. Fisting my cock, I shove myself back inside her and pull her to a seated position, facing me. "If this becomes too much... you need to tell me, because I'm going to mark you as mine. After tonight... your pussy belongs to me."

I grip her hips and rock her body against me, showing her how to move. Rhiannon finds the rhythm as she takes over, fucking my cock like she wants to own him. Her head falls back, and I can tell she's close to losing control. My hand slips up her front and my fingers grip her throat. Rhiannon stills for a moment, her eyes searching my own. When I let go, she grabs my hand and pushes it back to her neck.

"I'm close," she whispers, her hand tightening over mine.

My control snaps and I squeeze my hand tighter. Her throaty moan vibrates against my palm, and I can't stop myself from gripping her hip tighter with my free hand. Her palms are pressed into my shoulders as she rises and drops on my shaft. She swirls her hips, rubbing her clit against my pubic bone like a woman gone mad.

"*Fuck*," she mutters, her eyes closing as her pussy contracts around my cock. Her release is explosive, flooding my shaft with her juices as she cries out. I clutch her throat, choking her as she rides out her orgasm.

When she finally slows, I shift my hands and roll her off my lap, face down on the mattress. "Hold on, little dove... we're just getting started."

She squeaks when I jerk her hips up and shove my dick inside her. Her ass is perfectly round and begging for my mark. My palm smooths over the soft skin as I pause to relish in the feel of her wrapped around my shaft. I can't stop myself and slap my palm against her skin with a loud crack. She pulls away at first, but I thrust harder, tugging her against me as I do. "Your pussy is like silk." I slap her ass again, this time getting a throaty moan in return.

"I'm *going* to fuck you into submission, Rhiannon. A man like me needs control." My palm connects with the globe of her ass. "If you can't handle my needs, I'll set you free. But if you give yourself to me completely—I promise... you'll never want for anything again."

I thrust deeper, sliding my hand around to her front and finding her clit. Its swollen flesh begs for release as I press my thumb into the tiny nub. Rhiannon's core clamps down on my dick like a vise grip and I can feel my balls tingling with my release. "That's it. Let go. Let yourself fly with me, Rhiannon."

She cries out, her body tensing beneath me as her walls flutter around my cock. My dick swells inside her and my vision blurs as the most intense orgasm I've ever experienced rips out of me. The heat of my semen fills her womb, spilling out as I pound into her. I'm lost to the release, and I don't even realize I have her hair gripped in my hand. For a moment, I worry I've gone too far this time, but the look of lust and complete satisfaction that covers her face as she peers back over her shoulder has my dick semi-hard again.

"Where have you been my whole life?" I withdraw, pressing a kiss to her back as I slide off the bed.

"Waiting for someone to free me from hell." She throws an arm over her eyes and sighs as she collapses to her back in contentment.

I pause at the foot of the bed and stare at her. "I'm afraid I've freed you from one monster to deliver you into the arms of another."

I gather a towel from the bathroom and return to find her laying on her side watching me. She doesn't say anything as I step closer, and still, she's silent as I wipe away the remnants of our coupling. As I climb into the bed behind her, I notice the marks I left on her skin, and I cringe.

"*This* is why you shouldn't let me in." I trace the palm print coloring her ass. "I'm no better than your husband."

"Don't you *dare* say that." Rhiannon rolls over and pins me with a glare. "You are nothing like him. Sex is a weapon for him, Drake. If he doesn't get what he wants from me, he'll hold me down and take it. It isn't something I enjoy. What *we* just did..." she dances the tips of her fingers down my chest. "I've never felt that before. The way your fingers wrapped around my throat... the feeling of your hand across my ass. I liked it—a *lot*. What does that say about me? A woman who's been beaten by her husband for nearly ten years. I should freak out with the thought of what we just did. Instead—" she reaches down between our bodies and grips my cock in her hand. "I want you to do it again."

I grip her wrist, halting her exploration of my now hard dick. "I should've taken things slow with you. You're not really ready for the depravity I like in the bedroom—the pain I need to inflict on a woman to get off will scare you away."

"Are you saying you didn't get off?" She raises an eyebrow, knowing damn well I did.

"Of course, I did..." and then it hits me. She's the first woman I've fucked with no build-up through pain. Not only that, I fucked her *bare*. Something I swore I'd never do. "I've never had sex without a condom, Rhiannon. You make me lose my mind."

She bites down on her lip. "Are you mad at me because you broke your rule?"

I lean in to press my lips to hers, "No... just surprised." I push my fingers into her hair and drag her face to mine again. As I kiss her deeply, I roll her body over to her back and climb between her legs again. "And I can't seem to get enough."

This time when I push inside her, I do it slowly. I need to show myself that I can have her without the violence. As I pump my cock into her, her arms wind around my neck as she slips her tongue into my mouth. This kiss is powerful, yet tender. Even as she winds her legs around me, something about this time is different. My pace quickens as I chase the high of having her wrapped around my shaft. The feeling of her heat as our bodies slap against each other gives me a comfort I never expected to have during sex.

"Drake." It's one word off her lips, but hearing my name does something to me. "Oh, God… I'm going to come again."

Her warning sends me into hyper-drive, and I pick up my speed. My thrusts become erratic as my dick hardens even more inside her, then explodes once more. Her pussy sucks my cock in and clamps down, threatening to milk me dry. Together, we fall over the cliff of no return and shout out our release. My cum fills her channel, marking her as mine from the inside out.

Even as I pull out of this woman and roll to my side, tugging her frame against me, I know my entire belief that love destroys a man was wrong… because despite the worst possible timing, I am in love with her. The funny thing is I always believed love would destroy me… but instead it's the fear of not having the chance to love her or have her love in return.

"I promise you, Rhiannon." I brush my lips across her shoulder. "I will protect you from the evil out there… even if it means shielding you from the darkness, I have buried inside me."

"Don't hide the darkness, Drake. Let me be the light that banishes it."

Once more, with a single phrase, Rhiannon has totally obliterated everything I thought I knew. Tomorrow we will face the monster together... and no matter the outcome—I will make sure she's no longer a caged bird. Rhiannon will spread her wings and fly — even if it means I have to set her free.

For the first time in my life, I think I know what real pain will be like. Because the thought of not having her as mine guts me to the core.

15

Rhiannon

Waking up in Drake's arms is surreal. I shouldn't feel this connected to a man that I've only known for a few weeks, but I do. He's worried my feelings are misplaced, but I know they aren't. Even now as I sit beside him at the conference table waiting on Heath to get here, his hand casually strokes the bare skin of my thigh as a form of comfort. There's nothing sexual about it, which makes my heart open to him a little more each time his palm brushes over my knee.

"It's going to be okay." His voice pulls me from being inside my own head and I turn to look at him. "You're safe here. Archer is outside the door, and I will *not* let him hurt you, Rhiannon."

I nod, unable to speak thanks to the nerves that are clogging my throat. This will be the first time I've seen him since fleeing our shared residence weeks ago. The sound of raised voices outside the door has me stiffening my back and digging my fingers into the wooden tabletop. Drake stands just as the door bursts open and Heath strolls in, followed by two uniformed police officers.

"What the hell is *this*?" Drake barks, glancing at the two cops who look like they want to be here even less than we do.

"Mr. Winston." One of the uniforms steps forward and clears his throat. "Judge Carmichael has filed a police report that his estranged wife has stolen a substantial amount of money from their shared account after the divorce papers were served. Mrs. Carmichael." He steps toward me, and I can feel the blood drain from my face. "I'm afraid you're going to have to come with us down to the station."

"The *fuck* she is." Drake moves to block the officer. "I'd like to see the paperwork ordering my client in for questioning."

The officer hands over a piece of paper, and I watch as anger dances across Drake's features. "*Seriously*? You convinced one of your lackey friends to sign this for you?"

"Mrs. Carmichael." The police officer side-steps Drake and holds out his hand to me. "Please, don't make this harder than it needs to be. Once we get you down to the station, we can work this out."

"Okay," I whisper, slowly rising to my feet and forcing the tears to stay put. "Drake?" I look over to him, my body shaking with consternation.

"It's okay, little dove." Drake turns to the man waiting for me to step out. "I'll bring her down to the station. You—" Drake looks at Heath "—are not going to win this."

"He can't do that." Heath practically stomps his foot like a toddler not getting his way. "You have to arrest her!"

Drake's body thrums with irritation as he stares at Heath, "Actually, she can and *will* turn herself in, because she's not walking out of here without consult from me, her attorney. Gentleman, we will follow behind your patrol cars."

The officer nods in agreement. "Fine, sir, but only because we know who you are."

Heath practically throws a tantrum when he realizes he's lost this round, his hands waving wildly in the air. "This is *bullshit*. I want her in handcuffs and dragged out of here... right *now*. This bitch stole from me."

My gasp has everyone turning to look at me; everyone but Drake. He's moved so fast, no one saw him pin Heath to the wall -or stopped him. "You will not speak of her like that again. You've done enough damage to her, and I will not stand by and listen to you tear her down anymore. She is a person, not a possession."

"This is assault," Heath cries out as Drake releases his hold, allowing Heath to slide down the wall.

Drake growls, "Oh, if you want me to *assault* you, keep talking to Rhiannon as though she's your possession, Judge. I have no qualms making you feel the pain you've put her through— only you may not survive it like she has. Now kindly get the fuck out of my office or I will personally throw you out." Drake holds his hand out to me, which I willingly take. "Let's go, Rhiannon. The sooner we get down to the station, the sooner I can get you home and put an end to this fucker's charade."

Heath storms from the room, as we're gently escorted out by the officers. Drake hasn't said much to me, but I can tell by the way his neck flexes he's pissed. "Archer." He beckons his head of security over and grunts. "Find out how that mother fucker was able to get a judge to sign off on a bogus warrant."

Archer nods at Drake as he steps in front of me, his eyes filled with concern. "You, okay?"

"No. Not really." I whimper at the last word, still flabbergasted that my soon-to-be ex-husband has lied his way into having me arrested.

"We'll have you out in no time, Rhi. Hang in there, okay?" He grips my forearm as a show of support, before walking away.

"He's right, you know." Drake tugs me to the elevator and presses the down button. "Whatever angle Heath thinks he's working is going to implode and his ruse will be exposed."

"I believe you." I glance down at my feet, shocked that this is happening. I knew leaving came with risk, but I never thought for a second Heath would stoop to this level. The sudden stop of the elevator's descent has me jerking my eyes up just as Drake presses my body against the cool metal. The look in his eyes borders on feral, if not psychotic, and it makes me gasp at the sudden closeness of his body.

"I made you a promise and I'll keep it come hell or high water." His mouth covers mine in a needy kiss and I practically melt into him. His hands slip to my ass as he lifts my feet off the ground and wedges himself between my legs. "You don't belong to him anymore." He pushes his manhood against my center and steals my breath away with another heated kiss.

My feet hit the floor of the elevator and he presses the restart button, sending us down once more. "Heath *always* wins," I mumble, refusing to look at Drake. "I told you he uses his power to take whatever he wants."

"He's not taking you from *me*." Drake laces his fingers with mine and walks me to his car, easing me into the passenger seat.

No more words are spoken as we drive toward the police department, where I'll be turning myself in for a crime Heath concocted. I wonder if my parents are aware of what's happening, because I never even called them when I left. It was one more way for him to control the situation, and I wasn't willing to risk it.

"Rhiannon." Drake parks the car and turns to face me after killing the engine. "No matter what happens inside, know that I will not let them keep you. Archer is already digging into the arrest warrant, and I'm going to demand you be seen by another judge immediately."

"I don't look good in orange." I mutter as I stare out the window and say the most ridiculous thing possible. Drake snorts beside me and I cut my eyes over to him. "I'm serious, Drake. I wasn't made for jail and being here is already giving me hives. I don't know what Heath's planning, but this isn't it, I assure you. The last thing he's going to want is for me to be arrested and him to be embarrassed. So, whatever you have to do, do it."

The walk into the police station feels ominous, like a prisoner on death row walking to the chair and I can't stop the panic that's rising in my chest. Drake senses my apprehension and offers me comfort when he places his palm against my back. The woman at the desk is less than friendly when she buzzes us through and guides us down a narrow hallway to a large room.

"You'll need to wait out here, sir." She points to a row of benches outside the door, motioning for Drake to take a seat. "We need to process her, and you can't come back for that."

Drake gives me a hesitant smile and nods in understanding. "Just follow their directions, Rhiannon. It won't be long, okay?"

I nod, following the woman into the back room, my stomach twisting as the door closes, cutting me off from Drake. "Where are we going?"

"Oh, shut *up*." The female officer sneers at me, her tone curt and her body language bordering hateful. As soon as we step through a door at the rear of the room, I freeze. "I don't understand. Why is *he* here?"

"Rhiannon. Did you actually think you'd get away from me? I have more people than you can imagine in my pocket. This was easier than snapping my fingers." Heath demonstrates by doing just that as he steps forward and grips my arm with his fingers, the pressure burning into my skin.

I try jerking my arm out of his hold. "Stop. You can't do this —it's not legal, Heath. You'll go to jail."

He laughs, giving me a once over as he purses his lips in disgust. "I don't care. You're going with me and by the time that shit of an attorney figures out what's going on, he'll either understand the message that you're mine, or you'll be dead. One way or another you will belong to no one else— not even yourself."

"*Stop. Please.*" I try to pull away from him, but his strength is too much for me. My head swivels trying to find the officer who led me to my certain death, but she's gone, leaving only me and Heath. I try kicking and jerking against him, but the back of his hand connects with my face, sending my head into a swirl of blurred vision.

Somehow, we've managed to get outside, and Heath pushes me headfirst into his car. "Get in."

I tumble into the passenger seat, my forehead connecting with the center console. Between the pain radiating through my cheek, and the knot I'm sure is developing on my head, I can hardly stay awake. It isn't until I feel the motion of the vehicle, that I realize we're moving.

"Where are you taking me?" I whisper, knowing I'm trapped, and Drake has no idea.

"Somewhere I can teach you a lesson. You're mine, Rhiannon. The life you have belongs to me and eventually you're going to accept that, or death will be waiting for you."

I close my eyes, praying for a quick end. "I *hate* you."

"Hate is powered by love, my dear. And while you may never really love me, that's not an emotion I need to get what I want. Your body, your mind, and especially this—" he reaches over, shoving his hand between my thighs. "...is mine. I'll take what I want, when I want... *how* I want. Leaving was stupid, Rhiannon. It only angered me more. Part of me thinks I should have tossed you down those steps harder and saved me the trouble. But then... who would I have to fuck?"

I lean my head against the cool glass of the window as a lone tear slides down my cheek. Nothing in life is promised, not even my own freedom. I tried to save myself, but no one can beat the devil. I let my eyes fall closed as I conjure up a vision of Drake. For a moment in time, I had the chance to feel something more than hate... something more than fear.

My only regret is not telling him that even in the short amount of time I was falling for him. Now, he'll never know. I know with certainty that I may not survive this time. I know Heath will destroy me beyond repair—so much so, no man will ever want me again.

Who would want a broken mess of a woman?

16

Drake

I PACE the hallway like a caged bull inside the police station, my agitation mounting by the minute. It isn't until Archer arrives, wearing a mask of complete terror, do I finally realize my gut has been right and something is utterly wrong.

"What is it?" I don't hide the fear in my tone, causing Archer to jerk at my uncharacteristic reaction. He stops in front of me, his eyes wild with anger that probably matches my own.

"Where is she?" He leans around me, staring down the empty hallway looking for Rhiannon.

I wave my hand in the direction she walked. "I don't know. They took her to the back, and I haven't seen or heard from anyone since. I'm still waiting for the investigator to come out and talk with me."

"*Drake.*" Archer sighs as he fists his hair in his hand. "The fucking arrest was a sham. I've found where Carmichael forged the warrant. The judge listed on the bottom has no knowledge of the paperwork."

"Fuck." I growl, moving toward the door she went through eons ago. "I knew I should have made a call... how could I be so *stupid*?"

Pushing the door to the large room open, I'm not surprised to find it empty. Rage unlike anything I've ever felt courses through my veins and my vision narrows. Archer rests his hand on my shoulder, sensing my impending explosion. "Take a breath, Drake. We'll figure this out."

He guides me down the hallway, searching for anyone that can shed light on the situation. He stops when he finds a man who appears to be some sort of plainclothes officer, based on the suit he's donning. "Are you in charge here?"

The man's head snaps up from the papers he was reading through. His brows pinch together, and he gives us a look like 'who the fuck are you two? as he folds his arms across his chest tucking the folder beneath his arm.. "Who the hell are you two and how did you get back here?"

"I'm Drake Winston. I came in with Rhiannon Carmichael when two of your uniformed officers showed up with what we now know was a bogus arrest warrant."

"Whoa... whoa... whoa." He holds his hands up in front of himself as he shakes his head. "What the hell are you talking about? I'm Captain Davis, in charge of the warrants division, and I can assure you no new ones have come across my desk today. Are you sure it was a *warrant*? Or was it a notice to appear as a witness?"

"Look, buddy." I step into his space and growl in frustration. "The woman I brought in was escorted through those doors a half an hour ago. My head of security just got here and informed me the paperwork was forged. Now you've got two options." I inhale, letting the air burn in my lungs as I hold on to what little resolve I have left. "One—you can figure out who in the hell pulled this off and help us find the woman who's now missing. Or two... just go ahead and put me in cuffs right now because I aim to beat the ever-loving shit out of anyone who gets in my way looking for her."

"Calm the fuck down." He steps into me to exert dominance or something. "Someone has some explaining to do, but I'm going to need you to take a step back and chill. I don't know what the fuck is going on—but we're going to find out. Follow me."

Every nerve in my body is burning with molten hot rage, and all I want to do is wrap my hands around someone's neck and choke the life out of them. How could this happen? I'm one of the top attorneys in this city and I fucked up—and now Rhiannon is the one paying for it.

The captain motions for Archer and me to take a seat as he slides around his desk and lifts the phone to his ear. He slams the device down into the cradle and blows out an irritated breath. "No one seems to know what the hell you're talking about. Can you tell me the names of the officers who came to your house?"

I'm internally kicking myself because I didn't even ask. I was too focused on Heath and didn't bother to get any basic information. Something I would normally do. "No. I was busy keeping her *husband* at bay."

"Well, that's problematic." He leans back in his seat and frowns. "Whoever came to your house did it off the books. Which leads me to believe I might have some officers in need of discipline... or they were hired actors pretending to be officers. You didn't get any names... Did you get a badge number? A description?" I watch as he takes a couple steps back, a look of fear crossing his face as I growl with frustration. He lifts the phone from its cradle and speaks to someone about the situation. He shakes his head as he disconnects, equally disgusted with the turn of events. "Ok, I've reached out to internal affairs and they're going to pull the location data of all units in service today to see if we can get some details or leads. In the meantime, I'm going to locate...?"

I practically spit the bastard's name out, "Judge Heath Carmichael."

The captain's face blanches for a moment as he catches his breath, nodding his head slowly, "Oh shit. Well, if he was here, he's not now."

"So, *he* has her." My jaw tightens as I turn toward Archer. "Let's go. We need to find her."

"Mr. Winston." The captain stands up as we do. "Don't interfere with me or my people. This is now an active investigation."

"Captain. With all due respect, at least one person in your department is obviously in the judge's pocket and everybody else wouldn't know a goddamned thing was happening if I hadn't pointed it out to you. I don't plan to put my trust in people who would willingly walk a woman to her *death*." I grip the door as Archer, and I make our way out. I glance back at the captain, "You'll have to arrest me to stop me from bringing her home."

We make it into the hall before Archer grabs my arm, halting my forward momentum. "The captain was right about one thing. They're not here. And I've already got a guy at the Judge's house, Drake. They're not there, either."

My gaze pierces into Archer hatefully, "Dig into his life. The fucker has taken her somewhere off grid. Right now, I think it's time I pay her parents a visit." I head out, leaving Archer to scour the judge's private life for any information he can find—he's taken Rhiannon somewhere private, which can't mean anything good for her. Pressing the contact for my office, I get my secretary on the line and have her pull Rhiannon's file. Within minutes, I have the address to their place and the coordinates programmed into my navigation system.

Seeing me is going to be a shock because Rhiannon didn't tell them what was happening between her and Heath. She didn't want to bring them into the fold until she knew it was over and there wouldn't be anything Heath could use against her. Now I regret letting her make that decision.

They live just outside the city in an influential suburb—the kind with lawns just as pretentious as their owners. It's obvious as I glance around the manicured yards that her dad didn't want to lose his posh lifestyle, so he essentially gave his daughter to another man via marriage to keep his wallet fat. I wonder if he has any clue about the torment, she's endured just so he could keep up with the Jones'.

The driveway leads to a rather large house, way off the road. I want to gag at the ostentatious sight. I'm loaded and I don't care about flaunting for status quo—yet his fucking house screams 'look at me'. I waste no time parking in front of the main entrance to the residence and hop out. The longer this takes, the more likely she'll be lost to me completely.

My knuckles rap against the solid oak door, praying like hell they're both home. If anyone knows where he might have taken her, her father will. A man like him doesn't become controlled by another without some sort of gain—in his case, it was keeping his freedom by forfeiting his daughter's. It takes every ounce of willpower not to wrap my fingers around his neck when his face appears in the doorway.

"Can I help you?" Mr. Preston stares at me and though I see the recognition in his eyes, I can tell he's confused by my unannounced presence.

"I'm Drake Winston. We met briefly when my brother treated Rhiannon in the ER." I push past him and into the foyer, not bothering to wait for an invite. "Rhiannon hired me as her attorney. She's in trouble—and I need your help."

The soft voice that comes from behind me has both of us turning to face the owner. "What do you mean, she's in trouble?"

I recognize her from the hospital as Rhiannon's mother. Her face wears the lines of time and today in particular, they're etched in concern. "Your daughter fled her marriage several weeks ago. I'd given her sanctuary only to have her husband, Judge Carmichael, use his power to get her back. Now she's missing, and I'm certain she's in danger."

"Why did she need sanctuary?" Her father steps forward, his body tense with concern.

I want to laugh at his words, but I swallow the grudge I've formed for the man who gave life to the woman I have come to care about.

"Did you *really* not know?" I clench and unclench my fingers at my sides, trying to calm the beast threatening to rip out. "The man you gave your daughter to—the one you forced her into marrying—is a man that makes even *my* issues pale in comparison. Surely you didn't buy the bullshit that her broken arm was from an accidental tumble down the stairs, did you?"

The gasp slipping past her mother's lips makes me narrow my eyes at them both. "You've been so disconnected from your own child that you didn't know she was being beaten? What kind of person does that make either of you?"

"I..." her mother stammers, her eyes glistening with tears. "I always wondered if there was something wrong, but she never called."

My head shakes in disgust as bitterness courses through my veins at her response. "And don't you wonder why that is? Your daughter—the woman that willingly agreed to marry a man just to keep you out of jail—"

His gasp halts my words. "She... told you what happened? I didn't ask her to do it, you know. Rhiannon was stubborn and didn't want me to rot in prison for a crime I didn't commit. But Carmichael convinced her I was going to jail if she didn't."

"You gave her to a *monster*." I growl the words as they pass my lips. "He's been beating her for years. Not to mention *raping* her repeatedly whenever he wants. And now he has her again. I *almost* had her free—but that bastard played his game and has taken her somewhere. Which is why I am here."

"What do you need?" Her father crosses his arms over his chest, the anguish of my words is hitting him at his core, and I can see the myriad of emotions dancing across his features. His eyes glisten with tears as he swallows. "I never wanted her hurt." His voice cracks with regret. Beneath that though, I sense his fear. "I can't believe I didn't see it. Carmichael is a shady man and doesn't deserve to sit on the bench."

I nod, realizing he's been carrying guilt for this a long time. "Where would he have taken her?"

"I don't know." He starts down the hallway, "Follow me. I have a few things I can look through. Donna, try calling her and then Heath. Don't give away that you know anything but see if she will answer. I can't lose my daughter over something I never should have agreed to, Mr. Winston."

"You have my word… I *will* bring her home, Mr. Preston. I won't sleep until Rhiannon is safe in my arms again."

He turns to look at me, obviously realizing she *is* more to me than a client. "I thought you were her attorney."

"I am…" I grumble, trying not to deck him. I shove my hands into my pockets. "But I won't lie and say I haven't come to care for her on a personal level. It will not matter if I can't find her. Heath will do whatever he can to keep her away from me or anyone else."

"Let's dig through the information I have on him." He pulls open a massive filing cabinet and hands over a folder. "When I learned I wasn't actually facing jail time for embezzlement, which I didn't do by the way, I started digging. Unfortunately, the stuff I found didn't point to Judge Carmichael, even though I suspect he had a role in it somehow."

I flip through the contents of the manilla folder and groan. "Are you sure this is accurate?"

"Yes. I was going to share it with Rhiannon and let her make the decision to stay or leave, but every time I tried to talk with her—he was *there*."

"I can't get her." Donna Preston steps into the room. "She's not answering her phone, and neither is he."

Rhiannon's mother moves to stand beside her husband, who wraps an arm around her waist. "We'll find her, Donna. I promise you that. We should call the police." He gives me a pointed stare, to which I simply nod.

"It seems the Judge has some police in his pocket. They helped lure us down to the station under false pretenses. The captain over investigations is looking into the matter, but I'm not waiting around for them."

"Fuck." Mr. Preston sighs. "Donna, did Rhiannon ever mention a vacation home or anything?"

"No, but she mentioned his parents' place out in Winder. When his dad died, he left Heath the horse farm."

Sighing, I stare at them like they're idiots for not mentioning this sooner. "Where? Can you give me the address?"

"Um… yes. I think I wrote it down upstairs when she told me about it. Wait here, I'll go grab my notebook."

Taking several calming breaths, I tell myself over and over again that we'll bring her home… and when I do—the short time we've known each other means nothing.

Because I'm going to make her *mine*.

17

Rhiannon

THE LAST THING I remember is getting out of the car—rather, being dragged out of the car. I recognize my surroundings almost immediately and cringe. Heath has brought us to his family's horse farm, a location very few people know about. Tugging at my arms, I grunt when I'm met with the resistance from being tied to the four-poster bed in one of the rooms. My clothes—or what's left of them—lie in tattered remains on the mattress, putting my body on full display.

My eyes feel heavy as I blink the daze from my vision and try to look around the room.

"Ah... I see you're awake. Good. I was tiring of waiting for you to open your fucking eyes." Heath looks completely mad right now. He's pacing the floor, the entire time watching me with an evil glare.

"Why are you doing this, Heath? I don't love you—and I never have. The marriage was a sham from the start. Let me go and we can forget all of this ever happened."

"*No.*" He lurches forward and grabs my hair in his hand, pulling my head back as he gets in my face.

He growls as he speaks, spittle flying everywhere and landing on my face like he's some kind of rabid dog, "*You* will not ruin my life because you're a selfish cunt. If you leave, I lose the only thing that matters—your dad's company. Because if you walk, so will he."

My eyebrows knit together at his mention of my father. "What does my dad's company have to do with this?"

Heath rolls his eyes as he leans closer, dragging his nose along my cheek, his sandpaper-like tongue following, "*Everything*. But you were too dumb to ask questions and offered to save him... funny thing is, it wasn't even necessary. The threat of jail time was enough to make him sign over his life to me and my associates. You were just an added bonus. A bonus that could potentially destroy everything if that useless man, Drake Winston, starts digging around."

I don't understand what connection my dad's company could have with a judge—our family business is a shipping company. It was started by my grandad when he was in his twenties and passed on to my father when he died. "It's a shipping company, Heath. You're a judge. What in the hell could you possibly need with a business like that?"

Heath lets out a maniacal laugh that chills me to the core as he snaps his teeth closed mere inches from my face. "Not *me*, you stupid bitch... the man who lines my pockets to turn a blind eye at what he does for a living. And it's worked pretty nice, don't you think? It gave you everything you own, or rather, everything *I* own and let you have."

HIs fingers tighten in the strands of my hair, causing my scalp to prickle and me to hiss at the pain. "The only thing I've wanted is my freedom from *you*."

I regret the words immediately when the back of his hand connects with the side of my face. My eyes fill with tears and blur from the pain. *This* is the Heath I know—the Heath I've endured for nearly ten years. My eyes pop out when his hand pulls my head back and his disgusting fingers latch onto my throat. "The only way out is death, Rhiannon. I can play the heartbroken widow and keep your dad in my pocket that way."

"No." I rasp out, my throat burning with the lack of air. "He would know you did it."

Heath lets go of my hair, keeping his firm grip on my throat as he trails the fingers of his other hand down my chest, tapping them along my breastbone with a chuckle. "Not if I make it look like you killed yourself. Imagine their grief when they learn you took your own life because you're *so* miserable after bailing daddy dearest out. But *first*, I'm going to make you regret getting that *lawyer* involved."

I grunt as he squeezes my neck once more before he lets go and I follow his movements with my eyes as he strides toward the dresser and retrieves the handgun I hadn't noticed sitting there. He walks to the end of the bed and lays it down on the edge of the mattress beside my feet. I cry out in pain as he jerks my legs, stretching my arms that are still attached to the headboard with rope. At some point he removed the pink cast, which only makes the pain in my left arm even more excruciating—-so much so, I just get my head turned in time to vomit on the bed beside me. He doesn't seem fazed at my lax of decorum and yanks my feet again, putting my legs at an odd angle hanging over the edge.

"I deserve one last use of this pussy I own before I send you into the ground, Rhiannon."

Tears stream down my face as I press the lids closed and turn away from him. I silently pray for death to come faster. Heath has never been a kind man—not even in the bedroom. His use of sex has always been punishing and I imagine today will be no different. "Just kill me now, Heath. Fucking me alive or dead will feel the same for both of us. Cold and lifeless."

I grunt with the blow of his fist into my side. But he doesn't stop there, his fingers latch onto my exposed nipple, and he pinches with unforgiving force. My teeth dig into my bottom lip as I stifle the sounds of my whimper, because I know any indication of pain will make him more violent.

This time, there is so much hate behind his movements. If I didn't know any better, I'd think he's trying to kill me this way—especially when his teeth latch onto my other breast and bear down. This time I can't control the scream that breaks free, and as I'm expecting, it triggers a punch to my side again. Heath doesn't stop with one blow, though. He slams his knuckles into my flesh over and over again, breaking me one piece at a time. Even if by some miracle I survive this brutal ending, I'll be broken forever. My soft whimpers fill the room, mixing with his grunts as he slams inside me. His nails dig into the flesh of my thighs as he holds me in place, punishing my womb, wrecking it for anyone again.

"Please... *no more*." I break my silence, begging for the pain to be over. "Just kill me, Heath."

He covers my body with his, pulling my hair, ripping my scalp at the root as he jerks my head up. "Death is coming, Rhiannon—and it won't be slow like you want."

"Everyone will notice, Heath. Look at my body... at what you've done."

He laughs, twisting my head to bare my neck as he leans in and presses his lips to my ear. "When I tell them you took your life because of the secret life you lead... that these marks were from your secret lover, they'll buy your suicide. You aren't going to win—not against a God, dear."

"You're no God... you're pure evil and I hope when someone finds you, they make you burn in hell, where you belong." I spit the words, no longer fearing the pain. It's the only thing left reminding me I am human.

Heath jerks at my wrists in their confinement against the bed, the rope tearing through my skin as the knots are released. He pulls my ragged body off the bed by my hair, his hateful words resonating through me. "I'm fucking done with you."

He drags me, tossing me to the hard floor. The blunt force of his shoe connecting with the middle of my back causes me to lose what little I have left in my stomach, making him even madder. His leg continues its harsh punishment. The sound of my body breaking fills my head, pain radiating through my veins like a dark poison slowly beckoning me to my death.

I make the mistake of rolling over and the blows to my face are next. I can't raise my arms to protect myself out of sheer exhaustion, laced with the throbbing pain in my already broken arm. I can scarcely open my eyes when he finally steps away from my tattered frame pooled in a heap on the floor.

Blood drips down my skin mixed with tears I have no control over.

The sound of his footsteps and the door slamming tells me he left me to die. Any sane person would try to get out, but my body won't cooperate. Sharp needle-like sensations prickle against my skin with every breath I take, the agony threatening to make me vomit. That thought alone has me trying to slow the breaths I take, knowing if I retch, the intensity of my torment will increase tenfold. My body shakes with involuntary shivers and I'm not sure if it's from the bareness of my skin, or the physical damage to it. Even the cool feeling of the floor against my cheek is painful, but I can't move even though I want to. I don't know how much time passes because I'm caught in a dark vortex where neither exists and I cling to what little reality is left.

I have no idea how he thinks he'll pull off the lie that I committed suicide, not with the visible beating he's given me. But knowing Heath, he has something concocted in his twisted head to make himself look like the innocent victim in this fucked-up marriage. And since I didn't bother to tell anyone, I'd left him, it'll be his word against Drake's. Heath is a master manipulator—in court, *and* in life.

Just as I give into the darkness, the sensation of the rope being wrapped around my throat startles me into a semi-conscious haze. I'd wondered until this point how he was going to stage me ending my life, but it's no longer a question. I realize what he has planned and nothing I've endured with him—not the beatings or broken bones—compares to the terror coursing through my chest.

"Please." My whisper is so low, I don't think Heath hears me, but the slap to my face tells me otherwise.

"Shut up. Now that I've taken care of that stirring note you left me, it's time to put the full plan in action. First," He grips my hand, shoving something into it and closes his fingers around mine. "You need to sign your name to it, so it seems real."

There is no fight left in me—no resistance to push him away. Tears stream down my cheek, surely blending with the false words as he scrawls my name to the letter that will leave everyone devastated. The pen drops from my grasp as he releases his hold and steps away. The corded polyester scrapes against my throat like a twisted choker cutting into the tender flesh like a vice.

Heath returns and jerks the end of the death sentence, causing me to gag from the pressure it garnishes. My body slides across the hardwood floor, the rope tightening around my windpipe causing my hand to reach for it. Somehow, I muster the strength to lift my left arm that hangs numbly by my side and wrap those fingers around the rough loop as well.

"You won't be able to fight what's coming for you Rhiannon. No matter how hard you claw at the rope, your death is waiting."

Somehow, he manages to pull me all the way across the room into the master walk-in closet. Like the rest of this house, the ceilings are vaulted. And because it was owned by his parents, who were ranchers for lack of better description, the room is furnished with hooks and mounts for their various horse supplies—which makes this the perfect location for my demise.

He tugs the heavy brown cord with him as he steps onto the stool he apparently put in here earlier, loops an end through the eye hook mounted in the plaster above us, and drops it to the ground. His breathing is harried, and he grunts as he bends to retrieve the end lying beside me. Through the only eye I can open, I watch through blurry vision as he pulls it toward some kind of pulley mounted on the floor against the door.

"My dad insisted on having this in here. He didn't like leaving his prized saddles outside, so he always hung them in here. I always thought he was ridiculous for doing it, but seeing as it's coming in handy today, I almost feel bad for thinking it."

He threads the rope through the contraption's opening and clamp it down with the attached lever. "This *will* go faster if you don't fight it." He presses a button on the wall above the machine and the wheel starts to crank slowly, dragging me across the carpet. The fibers of the flooring burn across my skin as I grasp the loop around my throat, kicking my feet as if it's going to slow the end result.

"You should have stayed home, Rhiannon. Running away got you here. You really only have yourself to blame." The sound of the door is the only thing telling me he's fled the room. The pussy can't even watch as I strangle to death, proving he's as weak I pegged him for.

My body fights as I am slowly lifted off the ground, the rope constricting my esophagus with each inch I'm raised. My fingernails dig into my throat, trying to get between it and my skin. My legs flail as I come mostly off the ground, the rope threatening to snap my neck in two. The tips of my toes press into the carpet as I fight to keep my balance, preventing myself from pitching forward and snapping my neck.

I don't know how much time has elapsed, but my head feels like it's about to pop off with the slightest movement. And that scares me, because the fatigue is setting in tenfold in my legs trying to keep me alive. Not able to fight the exhaustion, the darkness starts to glaze over my eyes, and I can feel my feet going numb from the exertion it's taking to stay upright... my only hope keeping me from death.

As I dig my toes in, afraid to let go of the rope, my vision dots with black and I give in to the grim reaper standing before me. Just as I lose complete consciousness, the only voice I want to hear fills my head and I'm certain the last tear I have is shedding for him... *Drake*.

18

Drake

Archer tries to calm my nerves as we drive like a bat outta hell toward Judge Carmichael's parents' ranch. It's the only place he could have possibly taken Rhiannon in the amount of time that's passed. We haven't called the captain handling the investigation yet, because I want time to show Heath Carmichael what happens when you fuck with a Winston.

He should've known better than to tempt me, since he knows *exactly* who my father was. You'd think he wouldn't risk angering me. I might not be an exact copy of Calvin Winston, but his blood does run through my veins. And I will gladly let the darkness I've kept at bay out to show him exactly what I can do. His days of tormenting Rhiannon are over if I have anything to do with it.

Archer glances toward me, his eyes glittering with anger. "Don't go in there with guns blazing, Drake. I know you want him dead, but Rhiannon is going to need our help to get through this and being in jail won't let you be part of that."

"I can't promise anything, Archer. There's no telling what he's done to her in the hours he's had her."

Archer sighs as he pinches the bridge of his nose. "I get it. I just got a friend back, only to lose her to a man like him. I want him to pay just as much as you do but let *me* deal with him. You take care of her. *Please.*"

"Fine. I'll try not to kill the bastard, but no promises. If he *does* survive, you'd better make sure he regrets it. I want him to *know* who he's fucking with."

We turn onto the long and narrow path that leads to the Carmichael ranch. The property is massive, housing multiple barns and enclosures for the horses they once bred here. It used to be the place to go for horse enthusiasts, but when they died, leaving it to their only heir, Heath let the place go to shit.

"This place doesn't even look livable anymore. What the hell did he *do* to it?" Archer scans the grounds. "He'd have been better off selling the damn place to someone who would give a shit about it." He navigates the vehicle to the front of the gaudy ranch home, which looks more like a ranch and a mansion gave birth to a bastard and throws it in park. "I take it back. No one would want to buy this house - it's fucking ugly."

I slide out of the SUV and stand at the front end, waiting for him to get out. Archer is not going in without some kind of weapon, so seeing him go to the trunk and put on his shoulder holster isn't surprising.

"Don't worry, I've got my blade too." He smirks and lifts his pant leg, revealing the massive knife tucked into a leg holster.

When he confessed to being gay the night, he "met" Rhiannon, I have to say I was a bit surprised. He's the most masculine man I know, and I'd have never guessed he's batting for the other team. It pains me to think he hadn't told me before then, because it wouldn't have changed a damn thing between us. Archer is more than an associate—he's a friend.

"It doesn't look like anyone's here." I glance around as we climb the steps to the garish front door. "Is there somewhere else he could've parked his vehicle?"

Archer shrugs. "I don't know. Wait here while I walk around outside." He starts back down the steps and pauses. "I'm serious, Drake. Don't go fucking rogue on me now. We do this together or not at all."

I huff out my frustration but nod my head anyway. "I won't. Just fucking hurry, princess. We don't need to waste time."

Archer disappears around the side, and I move to peer into the window beside the door. There are no lights on, and it doesn't appear anyone is currently inside. I start getting antsy when Archer finally emerges from around back and confirms my suspicions.

"No vehicles parked in the back or in either of the garages. It looks like he either left or never came here." Archer takes the steps two at a time, stopping beside me. He tries the door handle, fully expecting it to be locked, but when it opens with ease, he shoots me a knowing look. "Guess he *was* here, unless they just don't give a fuck about squatters."

"No." I bark out, stepping toward the front entry again. "He has to have been here. Otherwise, Rhiannon's as good as dead."

He slips inside, with me hot on his heels as he reaches for his gun. "Let's clear the downstairs, then we can check up there." His hand motions to the steps leading upstairs.

The bottom floor consists of several massive rooms and a kitchen. All are open floor, making our investigation of the space quick. We only need to open a few closets to ensure the good judge isn't hiding anywhere.

"Drake." Archer places his hand on my chest. "You need to tell me you're ready to face whatever we find upstairs. If she's here and he isn't..." His voice falters. "I just need to know you can handle it."

"Let's just go, Archer. We're wasting time talking about my psyche. Will I be okay if we're too late? No. I won't—so stop yammering and let's go."

With the slight flick of his head, we start our ascent up the steps. Much like downstairs, there are several rooms up here —five, to be exact. Archer pushes open the first door to reveal a small bedroom. He steps inside, clearing the space, including the tiny closet. I blow out a breath and move toward the next door. Just like the first, it's empty. We continue this path through the remaining rooms, stopping at the last door at the end of the long hallway.

"You ready?" Archer scans me with concerned eyes. "Whatever we find, focus on getting her help."

"You two fuckfaces couldn't just let me do my job, could you?" The pissed-off voice of Captain Davis fills the hallway behind me. I glance over my shoulder to find his icy glare watching me as I wrap my fingers around the doorknob.

"How did you find us?" I grumble, my knuckles whitening as I tighten my hold.

"I called him." Archer says beside me. "When I walked around back, I had a bad feeling and knew we would probably need him here."

"Good thing too, because I don't need you fucking up evidence. Christ… you broke into a house, for fuck's sake." He scrubs his palm over his day-old stubble.

"Nope. The door was unlocked, actually." I smirk, knowing well and good that wouldn't hold up in a court of law, but truth be told—I don't give a flying fuck about rules right now.

The cop narrows his eyes at me. "Right. That's going to hold up in court. With me here, we can say I was following up on a lead. And you came along because Rhiannon is your client."

"Fine. Are we done figuring out things that don't matter?" I turn the handle. "Because this is the last place to check for my *client.*"

He growls under his breath as he holds his hands out like he's presenting us in our debut. "Go ahead. But *don't* fucking touch anything if we find something that can be used as evidence."

Archer nods and eases inside behind me. The three of us come to a screeching halt because there's no doubt Heath and Rhiannon have been here at some point. Her clothes lie in a tattered heap on the ground, and the bed is a rumpled mess. When I step closer, I can see the splattered evidence of blood dusting the sheets and I nearly lose my shit. "She was here. *Fuck.*"

A noise that sounds an awful lot like the ceiling caving in comes from behind the closed closet door. "Did you hear that?" Archer moves toward space, and like the captain, he has his gun drawn. Whatever made that noise sounded like an explosion.

"You ready?" Archer nods his head at Davis and opens the door.

All the air is sucked out of my lungs when we see what is waiting for us on the other side. Archer bellows something, but my ears are filled with the sound of blood rushing through my head. Davis halts Archer's forward motion momentarily and I watch from my stunned position as he takes out his phone, snapping pictures.

"Drake." Archer screams my name, snapping me from the alternate universe I'm trapped in.

My body moves on autopilot as I push past the two men and step inside. I've seen some fucked up shit in my life, but it was *nothing* compared to this. Rhiannon lays crumpled on the floor, a tattered rope pools around her lifeless body, along with fragments of the ceiling. My throat tightens when I see the other end of the rope connected to some kind of pulley. At some point. Heath had hung her, hoping she'd strangle to death, but my guess is her weight was too much for the rigging meant to hold no more than sixty pounds.

Her body is battered and torn from the beating she obviously took from Heath. Just the sight of her has me turning my head and bending over to puke the contents of my stomach onto the floor. Archer reaches around me, gripping her legs as he slides the blade from his pant leg.

"Drake. Fucking grab, her, *now.*" He balances her against him as he slices through the rope, allowing her limp body to collapse against mine.

I push past the agony and wrap my arms around her waist, whispering words I know she doesn't hear. "I got you, little dove."

I turn from the closet and rush out to lay her on the ground in the bedroom. Dropping to my knees beside her, I uncoil the rope from her neck and press my finger against her carotid artery, feeling for a pulse. Archer joins me on the floor on the opposite side, his hands balling into fists.

"I've got the cavalry coming. Is she alive?" Davis asks, watching us from his spot at her feet.

"Does it look like she's alive? She was fucking hanging by a noose and her skin is fucking pale." My tone is a bit snippier than I meant, but my head is a fucking mess as I lean down and cover her mouth with mine.

The last time my mouth was fitted over hers, it was for a very different reason. I'm on the verge of losing it and don't give two shits that my emotions are out for all to see. Tears stream down my face as I breathe air into her lungs, every breath I push past her lips, begging whatever God exists not to take her from me. Pausing, I watch as Archer presses into her chest, the rhythmic sound of his voice keeping me in the present as he counts out each compression. We fall into the routine, me breathing into her body and him forcing the blood into her veins.

I swear an eternity passes before I feel the palm of someone behind me press into my shoulder. "Let us take over."

Glancing up through tear-filled eyes, I slide back, giving the uniformed man room to work. Archer is watching with a broken gaze that matches my own, as the two paramedics fight to save Rhiannon. They scream something into the room—what I couldn't possibly tell you—and several other firefighters rush in. She's loaded onto a stretcher and hurried from the room, leaving me stuck in a trance.

"Drake." Archer is beside me, his hand tugging at my shirt. "Get up. They're taking her to the hospital. We've got to go."

My legs move on their own as if they're a separate entity lifting me from the floor and carrying me outside.

"Go with them." Archer shoves me toward the ambulance where the medics are loading her.

Mindlessly, I climb into the front passenger seat next to the fireman who has been tasked with driving, since both paramedics are in the back working desperately to revive her.

"How long was she down?" One of the men lifts their eyes to mine through the narrow hole that opens to the back of the rig.

"I don't know. We found her in the closet about ten minutes after arriving on scene. A stool was turned over beside her, so maybe she'd been propping her foot on it—but she wasn't breathing when we cut her down."

He focuses his attention back on her and I watch as they use the defibrillator on her again—for what has to be the third time. This time the sound of beeping fills the back, and its music to my ears when I hear the paramedic's voice come across the radio saying she has a pulse. It's like a dam being opened to release flood waters as my tears spill unabashedly from my eyes.

The driver presses his palm to my back. "This is good. It means there's hope."

I don't respond, I can't. The thought of watching someone else I love die, nearly guts me to the core. This is why I swore I'd never let anyone in again, but she tore through my defenses somehow and now the potential pain of losing her shatters my soul.

I tug the phone from my pocket and press the saved contact in my phone. "Meet us at Grady. Prepare your wife… it's not good." I don't wait for a response, I can't.

The ambulance makes it to Grady at lightning speed and I barely give the truck time to stop before I jump out. I'm there beside her gurney as they rush her inside the emergency room. A man I recognize from the Gala greets us at the doors marked staff only.

His palm presses into my chest. "Mr. Winston, you can't come back here. I promise… I'll do everything I can to save your friend."

"That's not my friend… that's the only woman I will ever love." The admission out loud shocks even me, but his quick intake of breath tells me he understands the significance of my words. Everyone knows the Winston brothers don't make attachments to people outside the family.

Archer appears out of nowhere and grabs my arm. "Come on, Drake. Let them do their job."

"Did they find him?" I cut my eyes to my friend as we head toward the emergency room waiting area.

"Yes. Captain Davis had men staking out his house and office. Seems the judge isn't as smart as he thinks. He thought going to the courthouse and hiding in his office would protect him. There's something else." Archer tenses beside me.

"What?" My jaw clenches and I'm not sure how much more shitty news I can take.

He clears his throat as he shoves his hands into his pockets. "The officers on scene found a suicide note from Rhiannon."

"*Bullshit*. Please tell me they know this is just another game… She wasn't trying to kill herself - she was trying to leave him." I drop into a plastic seat and press my elbows into my knees. I lace my fingers over my head and look down at the floor.

"Yeah. They know. Like I said, he wasn't the smartest man in covering his tracks. The computer he used at the house to type the damn thing still had the note opened in Word. His arrest is going to stick, Drake." Archer presses his hand against my shoulder and squeezes.

I shrug out of his hold, shaking my head as I say my biggest fear out loud. "Doesn't matter if she dies, Archer. It will be all for nothing."

"No, it won't. I showed you the evidence—he's tied to a man that will be brought down with him. It's a matter of time before we bring him down and all the shit that led him to doing this to her." Archer sounds convinced this case will be open and closed—but I know better. Things like this can take years, no matter how solid the evidence is.

"Drake." I glance up at the sound of my name, shock hitting me like a bullet to find my aunt standing in front of me. "Archer called me, son. I'm here for you." She squats down in front of me and tugs me into her arms. "You shouldn't have to sit here alone waiting to hear if the woman you love is going to make it."

My resolve crumbles again at her words, and for the first time since my mother's funeral, I sob like a baby.

19

Drake

Waiting is pure hell. I'm almost certain this uncertainty rivals seeing my mother murdered in cold blood by my dad. Rhiannon's mother sits on the right side of her bed, while I sit strategically placed on the other. Her good hand—if you can even call it that, is firmly held in mine, as it's the only connection I have keeping me sane.

She's required several surgeries since arriving in the hospital. Her neck is pinned with a halo, keeping her head perfectly still as the damage to her vertebrae heals. She was lucky the rope didn't cause a fracture to a place that would kill her instantly. The bruises are still angry and black, but those marks pale in comparison to the bite wounds that litter her body. Her left wrist, that had already been broken, ended up needing surgery after all. How she managed to claw her nails beneath the rope with her arm hanging as limp as it is a fucking miracle and possibly the only thing that saved her. Even seeing the splintered fingernails makes me sick to my stomach.

"She's going to pull through this. I know it." Her mother speaks, her voice scratchy and broken from the nights she's spent crying in this room.

"I know. She's stronger than she knows." I lean forward and rest my chin on the edge of her bed. "Little dove, you need to come back to me. You were right—you *are* the light to my darkness, and I need you to be whole in this lifetime."

Looking at her still form, I know I'd never hurt her the way my father hurt my mother. I'd die before I ever caused her pain. I realize the darkness inside me isn't really what I'd resigned myself to thinking it was. Instead, it comes from a place of fear and mourning over the loss of my mother—someone I loved very much. Her death is something I've never really dealt with before, despite the years of counseling.

"Mr. Winston." The calm voice of a woman pulls me from my thoughts, and I'm stunned to find my former client, Lori Conrad, standing in the doorway.

"Ms. Conrad." I force a smile at her, her presence confusing. Even though I know she's a nurse, I guess I hadn't realized she worked here. "What are you doing here?"

She steps inside and shuts the door, dipping her chin at Mrs. Preston. "When I heard the woman, they brought up here was your girlfriend, I asked to be assigned to her case. What you did for me has made such a difference in my life—I had to help you. I *will* say, it shocked me to hear you had a woman in your life, though. I seem to recall you saying you'd never get attached."

Rhiannon's mother's eyes are filled with questions as they bore into me from the other side of the bed. I shrug, "Then I met her. She turned my world upside down in a matter of days. I've broken every rule I had for myself because of her—and I'd do it again if she would just wake up."

Lori's features soften as she moves beside Rhiannon's bed. "Well, that won't be for a while. The doctors are going to keep her in a drug-induced coma for at least a week. And longer if her scans don't show improvement in her spine. But that's a good thing, Mr. Winston. Plus, looking at her chart, everything else looks good, for her situation at least. Her arm and body will heal, Mr. Winston. But her mind will take longer. Are you prepared to handle all that entails?"

I watch as she changes the fluids hanging on the IV. stand and adjusts some settings on the monitor. "I watched my own father beat my mother so badly she died from the blow to her head. And to make matters worse, my eldest brother had to be the one to end his reign of terror. So yeah..." I press a soft kiss to Rhiannon's hand that I'm still cradling. "...I can handle anything. This woman broke down my walls and I don't intend to walk away—ever."

The door opens, revealing my brother—Roland. He looks completely broken himself, but just the sight of him has me in complete shock, and I don't register the wetness coating my cheeks.

He steps into the room, followed by his head of security. "Hey. None of that, big brother." Roland steps forward and tugs me to my feet as he wraps his arms around me. I don't concern myself with the people in the room and let my emotions flood out of me as my younger brother consoles me.

"You came." My ragged voice cracks as I hold on to him like he's an anchor in a turbulent sea.

Roland's voice is soothing as he speaks. "Of course, I came. I wish I could have come sooner, but canceling my last show was a bitch."

Letting him go, I step back and blink at him in shock. "Canceled your show? Why in the hell did you do that?"

"It's a long story that I won't bore you with right now, and I can't stay long—I've got to get back and try to clear up a misunderstanding between Izzy and me." He looks somber when he says her name and I can't help but wonder if he has lady troubles of his own.

"Izzy?" I rub my forehead and close my eyes. "The publicist, right?"

"Yeah. But don't worry about me. Tell me about *her*." He nods his head at Rhiannon. "What are they saying?"

I move back to her bedside and sit down, tugging her hand in mine where it belongs.

"I had no idea you were related. I mean, I should have known, but wow." Lori blushes when we turn our eyes to her. "God, I'm sorry. You're here for your brother and I'm over here fangirling." She glances between me and Roland, her eyes filled with an unneeded apology.

"Don't apologize. Roland is used to the girls going ga-ga over him." I huff out a laugh as I press a kiss to Rhiannon's knuckles. "Rol, this is Lori Conrad. A former client and now Rhiannon's nurse."

He shoots her his classic boyish grin, causing her to blush. "Nice to meet you, though the circumstances suck."

"Yes, they do, and I promise to make sure I'm here every step of the way with your brother and her family. He helped me and now it's my turn to help him. But if you'll excuse me, I'll leave you alone for a bit. Mr. Winston?" She turns toward me, her serious expression back in place.

I look at her and smile. "Hey, I think you can call me Drake now—no more of this Mr. Winston shit."

"Right. Drake. If you need anything at all, press the call button. I'm here overnight, so it'll be me coming in." She pulls open the door and steps out.

"I'll walk out with you." Roland's head of security smiles at her, quickly moving out behind her. "I have some questions about her long-term care my boss asked me to inquire about."

I don't miss the blush on her face as she smiles gingerly at him. "Um, sure. Is that alright, Drake?"

His boss is Archer, so I know anything he is asking is for the case he is building against her shitstain husband. "Yes. Whatever he needs, give it to him."

My words have her blushing again as she stammers her response. "Um… right. Yeah. Okay, follow me."

"That was awkward." Mrs. Preston laughs, reminding me of her presence in the room. I'd forgotten she was sitting in the chair on the opposite side of the bed.

"Shit, I'm sorry. I should have introduced you right away. Roland. Meet Donna Preston. Rhiannon's mother." I motion my hand to the older woman.

"Sorry, we're meeting like this as well." Roland shakes her outstretched hand. "I was hoping it was for something grander. Like an engagement party."

I snort at his comment. "It's a little soon for that, brother. She doesn't even know how I feel, and she might not want that once she wakes up. Heath has robbed her of her freedom; I won't do the same."

"You don't look at her like a possession, like he did," her mother says with conviction. "You look at her with love. If she passes that up, I might send her to a mental ward."

I don't want her to pass it up, but I'm serious when I say I won't make her stay. "I won't force her. It has to be her decision and hers alone. I refuse to make her feel like she's broken free of one cage to land in another. She needs time to spread her wings and fly."

"Wow." Roland tugs an empty chair beside me and plops down. "You really *are* in love with her. The Drake I know *takes* what he wants."

Shaking my head, I scold him, "She's not a thing to take. Rhiannon is a person to want—and I want her unlike anything I've ever had before. It's going to gut me to let her walk away, but I will. She's shown me I was wrong. I *can* love… and it's her I want to give that love to, if she'll have it."

"Why wouldn't she want you?" Roland brushes his hand across her blanket covered leg. "You're a man who puts family first—I'm a testament to that."

I pin him with my gaze, a silent conversation filtering through the air. "You know why."

"That doesn't define you. Are you saying you and she… haven't…?" His eyes glide over to her mother, who's watching us intently.

"Please, dear God, tell me you have." She shakes her head. "The one thing she did confide in me was the lack of—you know. In the bedroom. A man like you looks like he can get the job done."

I blush as Roland erupts into a fit of laughter. The sound actually brings a smile to my face, and I shake my head. "We have."

"Once is all it takes for her to know if it's too much or not." Roland leans back in his seat and sighs.

I shrug, not sure how to put what I feel into words. "It wasn't like that, Rol."

"Interesting." He narrows his eyes at me. "You're telling me you had good ole-fashioned sex with a woman and liked it?"

"Jesus, Roland." I wave my hand toward her and her mom. "Think you could lay off this conversation out of respect for both of them?"

She winks as she walks past us. "Actually. I'll go grab some coffee and let you two hash this out. Though I won't deny I am curious as to what kind of kinks you have."

"Fuck *me*." Roland dies laughing again. "I bet your husband loves you."

Rhiannon's mom clicks her tongue at his statement. "If that were true, his sorry ass wouldn't have put us in this position, nor would he be in jail right this minute when our daughter needs him. By the way, thank you for providing your associate as his attorney. Maybe with Mr. Whitmire, Carl will manage to get off lightly."

"Alex is the best criminal defense attorney in the city. He'll probably have your husband labeled as a victim by the time he's done in court. Which… he kind of is."

"Right. I'll see you two in a few." She slips from the room, leaving us in privacy so Roland can continue grilling me, I'm sure.

"Her dad is involved?" Roland furrows his brows. "That's fucked up, brother."

I nod in agreement, "Yeah. It is. He let his daughter marry Heath to save his own hide. Turns out he's tangled up with Alessandro Hugo pretty deep."

"Wait… the same Hugo Gage is currently hiding from?" Roland's eyes widen at the sound of Hugo's name.

"Yep. The one and only." I growl in frustration at the mention of Gage. "Have you heard from Hugo again?"

Roland shrugs like it's no big deal. "Nah. Liam scared his man off pretty good."

"Speaking of Liam… he chased Rhiannon's nurse outta here pretty fast." I glance at the door.

Roland follows my line of sight and arches a brow. "Can you blame him? She's pretty hot for an older woman."

"Hey, fuck you buddy. She's not much older than me." I slap his shoulder in play, but my mood deflates the minute my eyes come to rest on Rhiannon again. "They say she's going to be kept in a coma for at least a week—so her neck can heal more."

"I hate Gage wasn't here to help you. He really fucked up."

I nod. "He has… but hopefully *this* mess will solve his."

Roland leans back in his chair and relaxes his frame. "We can hope. Now tell me about the woman who has thawed my brother's frozen heart."

"I actually knew of her in college—she was two years younger than me, so we didn't run in the same circles." I smile, thinking back to the moment I remembered we went to school together. "I ran into her at the ER the night we left your show. She was the patient Gage needed to tend to. I took one look at her and my chest clenched. I don't know if it's possible, but I think that was the moment I fell in love with her."

"Nothing's impossible, Drake. Sometimes, you meet a woman, and she knocks you completely off balance. You have no idea how to act or what to say, but you know without a doubt she's the one you want. I'm just glad you got a chance to show her what it could be like with someone who really loves her. Don't fuck it up when she wakes up. There's no guarantee of second chances." His expression says a thousand things and I want to ask what he means, but we're interrupted by the sound of his phone ringing.

"Fuck. I need to take this. I'll be back." Roland stands and hurries from the room. I stare at the closed door and wonder if *this* brother is hiding something from me, too. For now, I won't push—but when Rhiannon is well, he and I are going to talk.

I lean my head against the bed and blow out a frustrated breath. "Wake up, Rhiannon. You finally have your chance to fly, little bird."

20

Rhiannon

Two weeks later

My body feels like it's been run over by a cement truck and then tossed off a forty-story building. A metal contraption holds my head in place, keeping me from being able to look at anyone or anything except the ceiling. I'm stuck in a bed with a fucking catheter and bed pan as my toilet, adding to the frustration of being immobilized. Not to mention, I haven't seen Drake in a week.

He told me he loved me, and I fucking ruined everything. A panic attack set in, and the nurse had to give me drugs just to calm me down. I couldn't even explain why I reacted the way I did before he leaned in, kissed me on the forehead, and walked out of my room without uttering a single word.

My mother, who's been up my ass the entire time I've been here, won't tell me if he's called her to check in on me or if he's happened to've stopped by when I've been asleep— which is something I do a lot. Today is the first day my mom has left to go home for more than an hour or two, and I'm thankful, though the silence makes me nuts.

The doctor insists sleeping is needed as it's my body's way of healing—but I'm tired of being... *tired.* The doctor tells me, I suffered a traumatic event. Even thinking about his words, I can't help but snort still. Especially when I think of his face when I said something along the lines of *no shit, Sherlock, my husband beat me senseless then hung me with rope by my neck to kill me.*

Well, the joke's on Heath. I'm not dead... unfortunately, neither is he. Archer, Drake's head of security, and my best friend from college, has been by every day to check on me.

Archer explained why Heath was still breathing and what's happening to him. Supposedly, he got himself involved with a man named Alessandro Hugo. And Heath covers up Hugo's illegal activities in exchange for a pretty nice payment. My dad got sucked into the mess because of his shipping company. Hugo used Heath to threaten my dad so he could access his shipping barges to transport something illegal. Archer won't say what because it's still an ongoing investigation, but because of my dad's involvement, *he's* sitting in jail as well.

"Hey, Rhi." Archer's voice has me trying to turn my head toward the sound.

"Fuck." I cry out, more annoyed than hurt, simply because I can't do anything strapped down to my bed with this medieval contraption.

"Hey... stop that. We need you healed and trying to do dumb shit like that ain't going to make it happen. Besides, I brought you a present." He steps beside me, placing his face in my field of vision. "How ya feeling?"

"Like Frankenstein. I don't want a present. I just want this off and for…" I let my words trail off for a moment before swallowing down my nerves and asking, "Has Drake asked about me?" I bite down on my lip, feeling vulnerable all of a sudden.

"Actually." Drake's deep voice vibrates across the room, sending chills down my spine. *"I'm the present."*

"And now that my job is done, I'll be right outside keeping everyone out to give you privacy." Archer moves away, giving Drake room to stand beside me.

"You're *here.*" I blink, wishing I could pinch myself to make sure he's real and not a drug induced hallucination.

Drake takes my hand in his and strokes his thumb over the sensitive flesh. "I am. I'm sorry I ran out like that, but I needed some time to deal with the blow to my ego."

"Drake. You left before I could explain," I whisper, a tear seeping out of my eye. Drake reaches out with his other hand and swipes his thumb across my cheek, capturing the wetness gathering.

"Don't. You owe me nothing, Rhiannon. I should have waited until you were stronger. It was selfish of me to say I loved you so soon. It doesn't change the fact that I do—but still, I'm sorry."

"Please don't take it away." My voice cracks as I speak, a new form of panic emerging.

"Take what away?" Drake sits on the side of the bed, his arms braced on either side of my body as his head looms over my face.

"The words. Please… No one, aside from my mom and dad, has ever uttered them to me." I confess in rushed words.

"Little dove." He peers into my eyes. "I'll never take the words back. I'd say them every day if I didn't think it would send you into another panic attack. Seeing you hurt is not something I enjoy."

I swallow down my nerves, scared to voice my fears into the world. Aside from the shrink that visits me daily, no one else has been privy to them. "The panic attack wasn't about your words."

"Then what is it? You can tell me anything, Rhiannon. Nothing will change the fact that I'm yours." He shifts his weight, trying to get closer, despite the metal contraption around my head still.

I suck back a sob that threatens to rip free and hold my breath for a moment. "I'm scared I won't be enough for you. What Heath did to me—what you saw, plays on a loop in my head, Drake. What if I can't let you, or anyone for that matter, ever touch me again? That terrifies me more than death."

"First of all." He moves, covering more of my body carefully. His eyes bore into mine, his own soul reflecting in the deep pools of green. "There will be no other man *ever* touching you. When the time comes, little dove, that job will be solely mine. And I don't care if it takes days, weeks, or years, for you to get to that point. Now that I found you, I won't be walking away—ever. Do you hear me? I love you, Rhiannon. All of you. You accepted me and became the light I didn't know I needed. Now it's my turn. Let me be light to your dark. Let me show you what it means to be loved by a man.

Give me your heart, and I promise I'll guard it with my life, Rhiannon."

His words break through the wall I erected to protect myself from being hurt again... because I realize not having him would be the only pain I felt. This man fell into my life by mere chance and not once has he turned his back on me. He didn't let the fact that I was married to a monster stop him from taking a risk on me. And though I'm not ready to voice it out loud, I love him too.

"Ok." I close my eyes and sigh wishing I could turn back the clock of time.

"Fuck, I wish I could kiss you right now." Drake sighs, his frustration matching mine. "But I won't risk hurting you for my selfish needs."

"They aren't just your needs, Drake. But yeah... I think I'd like to wait until I don't smell like a horse's ass. These sponge baths don't really cut it."

Drake tries to hide his smile, but I see the twitch of his lips, anyway. "I think you smell fine."

"Are you sure you can do this with me? I'm broken, and I don't know if I can ever be whole again."

"I'm not completely sure I'm whole either. When I lost my parents, I was filled with so much anger and pain. I shut myself off from loving anyone but my brothers and aunt. Then you barreled into my life and everything I believed fell apart. When I saw you hanging there, another piece of me died. The only way I can be whole again, is if you're here with me. Together, we can complete the missing parts of each other. Just promise me you'll give it a chance—give *us* a chance."

"I promise." I blink the tears from my eyes and squeeze his hand. Needing to change the subject, I ask, "How're Gage and Roland?"

Drake sighs. "I don't know. This mess with Hugo has Gage radio silent—he's never gone this long without working. Archer talks to him and assures me that he's fine, but I still worry. And Roland?" He laughs. "He's not telling me something. He was supposed to be home by now, but instead he's run off to New Orleans."

"Why there?"

"Believe it or not... a woman, I think." Drake shakes his head. "Seems that the Winston men are being brought to their knees by the power of women."

"Good. You all deserve to be loved and loved back. What happened to you boys was a tragedy, but it shouldn't define you. Your dad is not you, or Gage, or Roland. It's about time you see that."

Drake narrows his eyes at me. "That's because of you. If these women can give them the light they need, then I'm all for it. I just wish Gage could have chosen an easier path. And Roland... I have no idea what his deal is. I just hope it doesn't involve a madman."

I giggle, happiness washing over me. "Aww... dealing with my soon to be ex-husband is too much?"

"Soon to be? Shit, I forgot to tell you." A smirk appears on his face. "The judge called me today. Your divorce has been granted. The courts didn't think you being married to him was fair. He tried to contest it but being on trial for your attempted murder didn't help his case."

"Oh my God. I'm not married to him anymore?" The air leaves my lungs. "This means I'm free?"

"Yes, little dove. You're free." Drake kisses the top of my hand he pulls to his lips. But I don't miss the underlying tone of sadness in his voice.

"Free to be with you, no barriers." His head snaps up to mine, his eyes unguarded. "I'm not ready for marriage… and I can't tell you I love you just yet—even though I am pretty sure that's what I feel. But if you'll have me, broken pieces and all, I'm yours."

He's about to respond when the door opens, and Archer pokes his head inside. "Sorry to interrupt, but the doc insists he needs to come in."

"Right." Drake moves to stand beside the bed. "Come on in."

Archer steps inside, the doctor right behind him. "Good news, Mrs. Carmichael."

"Actually, it's Preston. I'm officially divorced." I smile as the words spill out.

The doctor chuckles, "That's fantastic. It's going to make this next news even better. I got your scans back. Your halo can come off today. You're going to be able to get out of that bed and start some physical therapy. To gain some strength back."

I cut my eyes toward him, needing to see the truth in his face. "Really?"

"Yep. The nurse will be down to get you and take you into the OR. While I could take the thing off here, I'd rather do it in a more sterile environment. Shouldn't take longer than an hour."

"Maybe you could go get me some real clothes." I tug on Drake's hand. "And a brush."

He lets go and moves to the makeshift closet, pulling it open to reveal clothes hanging on the inside. "Already did that, baby."

"Already taking care of things." I laugh. "Well... let's get this show on the road. I want to see my feet and take a hot ass shower."

"Well, don't get ahead of yourself. You still can't shower. You're entirely too weak and are a fall risk." Archer snickers from his place in the corner of the room and I mentally visualize punching him in the dick.

Focusing my thoughts on the doctor, I whine like a toddler about to go into a full-blown tantrum. "No... please, I'll do anything. I'll sit on a stool or let them push the wheelchair in there for fucks sake."

"I—" the doctor starts to object, but Drake cuts him off.

"I'll get in with her. Make sure she's safe. Please, she *needs* this." He tightens his hand in mine.

The doctor seems to mull over his offer, his eyes flicking between the two of us. "Fine, but you need to sit on a shower chair with her. If she falls, all the healing to her neck will have been for nothing." He turns to me. "I'll go ahead and take out the catheter to give you some dignity, but you'll need help to get to and from the bathroom as well."

I arch a brow and grin. "He's got me, doc. I'm not going anywhere."

He laughs, shaking his head in defeat. "You're a lucky woman. I'll send in the nurse."

"Wow, you two are something. I'm not sure what, but *something*." Archer laughs at the exchange. "I'm going to head out. I'll be back in the morning for you, Drake."

"Bye Archer." I call out as he slips from the room, then turn to Drake. "You're staying tonight?"

"Forever, Rhiannon. I'm staying forever."

21

Rhiannon

IF YOU'D HAVE TOLD me I'd be standing inside an apartment that belonged to a man that loved me more than his next breath after my husband tried to kill me, I'd have said you're an idiot. But that's exactly what I'm doing. After my halo came off and the doctor told me I could go home with a home healthcare nurse, Drake didn't waste any time—he offered Lori, the same nurse that had been helping me throughout my hospital stay, enough money to take a leave of absence and be my personal nurse. Of course, the sizable donation he made to the hospital helped him get what he wanted.

Now, I'm here, easing myself into the bathtub, something that will certainly get me a lecture when Drake finds me. He still refuses to let me do anything alone—despite the fact I'm way ahead of where the doctor expected me to be in physical therapy. Granted, I still get weak moments on my own two feet, but I really want to be able to do things myself and the frustration of having things done for me all the time is mounting.

"Rhiannon. I asked you to wait on me." Drake steps into the bathroom, and his head tilts when he sees me already beneath the bubbles. "You could have slipped and done something to hurt yourself."

"Drake." I close my eyes and bark out his name, regretting the tone of my voice instantly. "I love you, but damn. I just want to feel like I'm human. I need to do things on my own or I'm just another weak little girl who needs everyone doing everything for her."

The silence is deafening, and I worry I've gone too far, so I crack open an eye. Drake is standing perfectly still, his eyes frozen on my face. "Are you okay? I'm sorry I snapped but—"

Drake moves faster than I can blink and drops to his knees beside the tub. "You love me?"

I hold his gaze, confused at his question. "Huh?"

"You said you loved me." He threads his fingers through my hair, careful not to pull on my neck too hard. "Just now. You said, 'I love you, but damn'. Then whatever else followed, but in those words, every other thing out of your mouth fell to the wayside."

"I—" I furrow my brows. Shock courses through my veins when I realize what I just voiced without a second thought. I hadn't said those words to him yet, because I wasn't sure if what I felt was really love. But when I think about the man kneeling beside me, I know the pounding in my heart isn't anxiety or fear. No... it's exactly what I've been afraid to acknowledge out loud. I love him, and I'm done fighting it. "I do. I love you, Drake. So much it scares me."

"Scares you? Loving me should elicit a lot of emotions, but not *that* one."

Chuckling softly, I can't help but smile, "Not in the way you think." I reach my hand out, pressing my bubble-clad palm to his cheek. "I lost so much time with a man that treated me like shit. The way you love me is unlike anything I ever thought I'd have. It overwhelms me, but in a good way. I worry I won't love you the same, and *that* is what scares me."

"Love me however you can. Give me whatever you have, Rhiannon. I'll take what I can get from you. And one day… when you're ready—I'm going to put my ring on your finger."

"I love you, Drake. I promise that won't be too far away." I rub my thumb across his cheek. "Take a bath with me?"

He groans, his eyes closing in frustration. "Rhi. I don't think I can do that. Not yet."

"Please." I whisper my plea. "I need to feel you against me. I need to know what happened to me hasn't turned you off from being with me—and I don't mean sex. Not yet. I don't know when I'll be ready for that. But I need you to hold me somewhere other than in bed. I know you wait until I'm asleep to pull me close, but I'm not going to break if you hold me now."

Drake blows out a defeated breath and I know I've won the battle when he steps back and begins shedding his clothes. "Fine. But no touching me. A man only has so much restraint and I haven't gotten off in months."

"What?" I gasp at his admission. "Not even alone?"

"Not even alone? You say that as if I would be with someone else." He cocks his eyebrow at me, pausing as he unbuttons his pants. "You don't think I'm getting sex elsewhere, do you?" I turn my head away from him. "Rhiannon, look at me."

I turn my head and bite my lip. "I know you used to go to that sex club."

"I haven't been there since the night I had a taste of your pussy, little dove. You've ruined me for all other women."

"I can't say I'm sad about that. But still." I take a breath, watching as he starts to push his pants down, revealing his fitted boxers beneath. "You're a man—who up until me had a big sexual appetite. I didn't really expect that to change…"

"Not big. Just *different*. I used the club for sex that let me keep the darkness I thought ran through my veins at bay." He pushes off his socks and motions for me to slide forward. Once there's enough room behind me, he slides in, boxers and all.

"You're leaving them on?" I lean my head back, peering into his eyes.

"I need something to help me control my *sexual appetite*." He throws my words back at me.

I flinch, worried I've hurt his feelings. "I didn't mean it in a bad way. I'd hoped we would be exploring plenty of sex together—until this happened, anyway."

"Until you, I liked my sex meaningless and controlled. What I got at the club isn't something I want with you, little dove. With you… I want it all. All your fantasies. All your firsts. All your love. That isn't something a sex club can give me."

I don't speak. I can't. The truth in his words has my heart hammering inside my chest and I don't want to ruin the moment by telling him I don't know how to give him those things. Instead, I snuggle into him and just let him hold me. We spend the rest of our time talking about the case coming up with Heath and how he's worried about his siblings. When we finally crawl out of the water, our skin is wrinkled and the water's cold. Drake wraps me in a towel and scoops me into his arms. I start to protest but stop when I realize it isn't because he thinks I'm weak. It's because he can't stand the thought that I might get hurt right now.

He helps me dry off and tug on a pair of leggings and an over-sized shirt. "You hungry?" He kisses my lips, pulling me against his bare chest. I lean my cheek against his skin and trace the lines of muscles with my fingertip.

"I could eat." I nod my head against him. "Do you think the trial will go quickly?"

"No. Unfortunately not. With Alessandro Hugo being tied to it, the process is going to take longer. If they can get Heath to turn in state's witness, it might go faster. But the judge presiding over his case doesn't want to give him a lighter sentence just to get him to agree."

Archers already told me that the judge hearing the case was a hardass and he's especially disgusted with the fact Heath had been a judge himself. The FBI's now involved, and it doesn't look like Heath is going to help without something in return. I hate every minute of it being dragged out.

We start toward the kitchen when Drake's phone rings. He pulls it from his pocket, his free arm wrapped around my shoulder as he does.

"Hey." He smiles down at me, but I watch as his face morphs into sheer panic. "What do you mean? Is he okay? Okay...

Fuck. Keep me posted. Rhiannon and I will get dressed and head your way. Yes... we're coming. That's my fucking brother, Archer. I don't give a shit."

He shoves the phone in his pocket and steps away from me. I watch as he rubs his hand over his face and lets out a guttural sound of frustration.

"Drake." I rush toward him as fast as my gimpy ass will carry me, grabbing his hands which are covering his face. "What is it? Talk to me, baby."

His eyes focus on me, and he blinks. "It's Gage." He swallows, unable to find the words.

"Gage? Is he hurt?" His eyes are unfocused as he stares at me. "Drake... fucking say something."

"You know he shot my dad." He whispers the words. "It closed him off to all of us for years. Then one day, he was just Gage again."

I squeeze his fingers in mine. "What does that have to do with anything? I don't understand."

His body stiffens and he takes a deep breath. "Alessandro Hugo is dead."

"*Dead?*" I blink at the shocking statement. "What does that have to do with Gage?"

He closes his eyes, his body tensing up with each breath. When they finally open to look into mine, I suck in a breath at the utter loss I see reflecting back at me.

"Because... Gage *shot* him."

Gage might be the man who heals the sick… but that doesn't mean he won't do anything to protect the people he loves— even if it means killing someone.
https://books2read.com/Bad-Diagnosis

Playlist

Bad Guy—Billie Ellish'

Mr. Bad Guy—Freddie Mercury

Hooked—Why Don't We

Ain't My Fault—Zara Larson

Rock Bottom—Hailee Stienfield

I Wanna Fuck You—Snoop Dogg

Lonley Together—Avicii, Rita Orr

Personal—HRVY

S&M—Rhianna

Confident—Justin Bieber

Back To You—Selena Gomez

Treat You Better—Shawn Mendes

Fixed—New Hope Club

I Wanna Be Your Slave—Maneskin

Run—Joji

I Fall Apart—Post Malone

Arcade—Duncan Laurence

Creature—Jelly Roll

Nothing Left At All—Jelly Roll

Supernova—Ansel Elgort

New—Day

Infinity—Jaymes Young

Flames—R3HAB, Zayn

Monster In Me—Little Mix

Follow My Playlist On Spotify @NerdyDirtyBooks

SPECIAL

Acknowledgments

Special thank you to Lux Miller for her amazing wordsmith skills. I am grateful to have her as part of my inner circle, because without her this book would have killed me... so I probably owe her a kidney.

And to my husband, thank you for not divorcing me or smothering me at night when I was working instead of sleeping.

ABOUT

Dori Pulitno

"Welcome to the dark side. We have sexy Mafiosos."

Dori P is the naughtier, much dirtier half of USA Today Bestselling author, LC Taylor. The bad girl Dori embraces her Italian side with heroic hitmen, decadent conflicted dons, and oh so f*ckable assassins trying to trade their devilish ways for salvation and the perfect woman to tie to their bed.

And F**k following the rules… this author is most definitely trigger happy.

Sign up for Dori's newsletter and never miss a new release.
www.authordoripulitano.com